Liars, Lifters, & Piracy

Book I of III

from the upcoming novel

Temple of Lost Tears

Vol. 1

(Pulp Edition)

By Nicholaus C. Hutton

Published by NIXPLOTS.COM

ISBN: 979-8-9991088-4-5 (PULP PRINT)

Cover design by Nic C. Hutton

Edited by [optional]

Printed in the United States of America

First Edition

UPCOMING RELEASES

BOOK I Liars, Lifters, & Piracy (this book)—Halloween 2025

BOOK II Lost Gift on the Ocean Floor—Thanksgiving 2025

BOOK III Barrel of Snakes—Christmas 2025

Complete Novel: Temple of Lost Tears 1st ¼ 2026

Chapter One

Brew to Brawl

Mud clung to the boots of the regulars who made their way into The Hairy Barrel early this evening. Manure stench crept in with each patron as the stables, most would agree, were far too close to the entrance. Heavy rain clouds rolled away, continuing to drench other dry lands beneath them. As mist rose between the damp branches, the sun brightened the woodland area for the last hour before it dipped, dimmed, and disappeared, until night fell, swallowing up the land.

The barkeep did his menial job, picking up fallen chairs and wiping down grimy glasses from the night before. He took little notice of a traveler waiting to be served at the bar whose stained cloak suggested he could use a drink. Regulars helped themselves to the only barrel of brew found in the tavern's center. The brew's stench would make any high elf gag, unfit for more popular towns or cities. However, it suited these folks just fine.

Noticing that the stranger continued to wait patiently, most likely for something he could stomach, the barkeep took his time serving him. He often dealt with outsiders who strutted in like they owned the place, so he milked the fact that they were dependent on him and not the other way around. Seeing the stranger waiting contently, the barkeep finally dropped his rag and welcomed the traveler with the cheeriest greeting this place could muster.

"What do you want?"

"I'll take any dark ale you have." The stranger nodded toward the back of the bar. "I'm familiar with those dwarven barrels. I'm sure I'll be pleased with whatever they hold."

"Haven't served that in a while. With low demand and my cost, most can't afford it. Five reds."

"My travels are allowing me to spoil myself. I appreciate it."

The barkeep's eyebrow raised. "Mm hmm."

Marx was the stranger's name. Black hair came down like icicles over the top part of his head. His green eyes, speckled brown, matched the forest. Tan skin spoke of sunlit roads while the lines around his eyes gave away his age of late thirties. Beneath his dirt-smudged cloak, fine blue silks were hidden. Although not wealthy, he enjoyed the comfort of loose-fitting, fine fabric that brushed against him with each stride. Here, he was glad to hide them in the company that surrounded him. Strapped to his side was a blade with a strange handle, unusually longer than the blade itself. Marx stacked five copper coins just as the barkeep came back to make the swap.

"Enjoy," the barkeep said expressionlessly.

"Many thanks." Marx brought the glass up to his lips; a slight sniff assured it was halfway decent.

As Marx turned, he found a young woman who had just sat next to him. She wore green overalls over an off-white shirt with frills that hugged her shoulders. Her clothes appeared fine in the tavern's dim light, but a longer glance revealed frayed edges, and the scent of broken leaves whispered days, perhaps weeks spent out in the forest. Strands of brown hair played with one another, tumbling as they dropped around her face, landing on her shoulders. Her bright, almost yellow hazel eyes scanned his features before resting with his gaze. She smiled half-heartedly, setting the bait that suggested times had been tough.

"Never seen you here before," she said.

"Never been here before," Marx replied.

"What brings you out here?"

"I was just asking myself the same question. I tend to go where the wind takes me."

She replied with a genuine smirk. Something told him she, too, lived a similar life.

"Name is Marx, and you are?"

"Kara, nice to meet you," she said with a sly glint. "You gonna offer a girl a drink?"

"Are you old enough to drink?"

"Not that I have to be way out here, but yes, for your information, I'm nineteen," she replied coolly.

"Although you may be old enough to drink, you're not old enough for me." He placed two steel coins on the bar. "This should buy you a night's worth of that raw swish. Good day." He nodded farewell and walked away.

Glad she got what she came for, Kara walked behind the bar, grabbed a glass, and hollered at the barkeep. "Vonnie, coins on the bar."

"He didn't try to keep ya? Ha!" Vonnie smirked.

"It seems there are *some* good men out there. Coulda fooled me." She walked to the barrel in the center of the tavern.

Marx found a table in the back corner, barely lit as the tavern's lanterns failed to reach that far. Reaching into his pockets, he fished until he found a used candle. He lit the wick, placed it to his liking, and opened his journal. He hadn't found the time nor the dry atmosphere to jot down what had happened in the last few days. The tragic ending of his canine companion delayed his desire to record such a painful event.

Recalling the time before the storm, he thought about a new, strange feeling lingering in the air. Like a horse fly pestering a napping man, the feeling never left him alone too long. Still, he was unsure how to articulate it properly. Was it the silence after rumors filled the room, of armies gathering in the corners of the world? Or was it the division of the new religions pulling families and friends apart? Like his dwarven comrade's. Their views changing so suddenly, a jarring shift for the traditional mountain dwarves. He had no evidence or coherent claims, just a feeling—that the world was ready to rattle off its axis, that, and he noticed his hand found his hilt more often each day.

Feeling around for the last thing needed, his pen, he discovered the nib was damaged, bent beyond repair. Although he couldn't identify the discomfort he felt, a smile rose, for he was sure, as he was in every situation, the nib had broken for a reason. It allowed him to take the night off from his journal and his worries. Placing everything back in his pockets, he ensured that one item, an emblem attached to a necklace, was still with him. He pressed his fingerprints up against the sharp edges of the engravings. Feeling its coolness, the emblem steadied him as he blew out the candle, sat back, and observed those who dwelt around him.

Kara greeted a young boy with a shake of his shaved head. The boy had to be around twelve; a skinny frame and filthy clothes told of a humbling life. He had a wooden sword strapped to his side. Marx listened in.

"Come on, Ethen, you can sip off mine. Vonnie won't know and probably doesn't care. This fermented urine doesn't cost him much of anything and you know there's no guards around here. Come on, let loose." Kara brought her glass to his face as he shoved it away.

"We're supposed to check out the recruitment tent tomorrow morning. Did you forget?"

"No, I didn't forget. They're having a listing all day at Laneloon. You know, little brother, I wrote a new song today. This is what *I* dream about."

Ethen rolled his eyes.

"You know I don't want to join some stupid army." She took a drink, fighting back the taste, she swallowed twice. "I want to write songs all day."

Ethen turned away before reengaging. "We already talked about this. Writing songs won't feed us. We need a real job. I'm tired of living off scraps of food every day. They will pay to train us. Then we can leave, become mercenaries. People will hire us just to escort them around the world."

"Or we can die on the battlefield, on the *first* day, fighting someone else's fight."

"So, all that talk the other day was just lies?"

"No, I just didn't think it through."

"You never think anything through," Ethen scowled.

"Like running away to take care of you?" she returned sharply.

Their faces softened with regret.

"Look, I'm sorry. We'll go to Laneloon Harbor tomorrow to see what they're offering. *If* you take a drink and listen to my song." Kara brought her cup up again.

No more than a moment passed before Ethen broke his silence. "I'm sorry too," He took Kara's glass. Squinted eyes and a stretched frown seemed to be the right response to the swish.

More folk filled the small bar. Marx was surprised by how many found this place. Not only that, but he figured only humans would wander here. A hill dwarf entered followed by a troll who got stuck in the doorway. Others gathered to pull him through as if this was a daily routine. As rare a sight as those were, what he saw next was astounding.

A lily elf accompanied by a goblin. Both sworn enemies by nature and by history. Lily elves were smaller than their cousins, and their pointed ears much larger by comparison. Standing about three and a half feet tall with their ageless features, they resembled children. From what Marx had heard, most elves shared a noble and well-mannered behavior and wouldn't be caught dead in a place like this. Still, the goblin was the most curious thing.

Goblins were usually killed on the spot. Although small, they're immune to pain, fearless, and don't mind fighting to the death when provoked, which took as much as an awkward glance. These traits alone were reasons to kill them quick and get it over with. On top of that, the goblin's homeland was on the other side of the world. Marx thought how glad he was to take the night off from his journal, as this was becoming quite the show.

The unlikely duo sat at Kara and Ethen's table after they too got their glasses full. Soon, the crowds talked over each other as the barrel of brew in the center emptied. Pipes and rolled cigarettes filled the tavern with stale smoke. Marx watched the hill dwarf join Kara's table to play a game of cards. After a few hands, the dwarf made a motion to Kara. Marx wasn't sure what was asked, but Kara kept shaking her head in refusal. Finally, a smile from Kara was followed with a nod. The dwarf stepped on top of the table and boomed his voice over the noisy crowd.

"Quiet, the lot of ya! Kara's gotta new tune and I fer one, wanna hear it. What say ye?" the dwarf yelled.

The crowd cheered in agreement.

"Good to hear. Lass? Ye got it from here?" He grabbed her by the wrist and easily lifted her up as he got down.

"Okay, I just wrote it today, and I kinda wrote it for all you scumbags." Kara shouted across the bar.

The crowd laughed.

"Okay, I'll need your help. When I stomp like this." She stomped. "You all need to stomp too. And if you break anything, you buy it."

"You got that right!" Vonnie hollered.

Kara took out her pan flute and played a song that ended with three notes repeatedly. As she played, she let the crowd know when to stomp while getting the tune stuck in their heads. After they got a feel for the beat, she sang.

"In the night … misfits creep, to meet … a darkened feeling.

That the day… never stayed… long enough to offer healing.

Blades are raised… dice are rolled to raise the stakes.

The fiends seek… peek and sneak… achieving their dreams to…"

She jumped from one table to another and raised her foot. The folk followed her lead, raising their hands over their tables.

"Plots to cause the good to rot.

Schemes to tease the good to leave.

Lies to convince the good to die.

Abuse to ruse that the good will lose."

She slowed her pace to match the new shattering tempo.

"Steal for the sake to take.

Kill at will for the thrill.

Why so bad, some will ask…

Because the bad got nothing better to do!"

She repeated the chorus while the crowd caught on and sang in as well. Soon, the entire tavern joined.

"Steal for the sake to take.

Kill at will for the thrill.

Why so bad, some will ask…"

The entire tavern yelled together, *"Because the bad got nothing better to do!"*

Everyone laughed and clapped as Kara played her flute, hopping around the tavern. She ended up standing on the bar to tell the ending.

"As the night begins to lose in sight.

The day comes to take away.

And for all the bad, I'm sorry to say…,

the good will triumph any way."

"Aww," the crowd playfully groaned.

She played one last short flute solo before singing, *"Good day."*

"Sorry fellas," she said with a smirk and shrugged shoulders. Jumping down, she received praise all the way back to her table.

She spotted Marx, who raised his glass of ale as she sat down by her brother. Marx shook his head, fascinated when the goblin grinned, showing his enjoyment by welcoming Kara back to her seat. He'd never seen a goblin smile before, much less show appreciation.

"Truly remarkable," Marx said to himself as he took a sip.

The entrance swung open, and a woman stood in the doorway. She seemed to regret entering as soon as she looked at the room that looked right back. She had to be in her mid-twenties. Overdressed in this place, she wore a yellow dress with embedded black rhinestones at the bottom. Dark red hair matched her dark eyes along with light brown skin. The lantern's flames brought light to every crafted curve to her face, both soft and sharp. She was striking, not just compared to this lot, but to all of Iris.

She took another glance around the room. Her dark eyes, still hidden in the tavern's dimness, found Marx's. Whether she smiled at him or not, he wasn't sure. She left almost as swiftly as she entered. When she did, the lantern's glow dimmed even more, or so Marx thought. A moment passed. Something didn't sit quite right with him. Although the song Kara sang was more playful than not, it had some truth to it. This small tavern was far away from any capital, city or town, just as it was far from the law. He was planning on checking on his horse after finishing his drink already. However, he figured he'd wait another moment or two, not giving the impression he was chasing after her.

He slowly finished the last quarter of his ale and stood up. When he made his way to the door, Kara approached. He could tell she was tipsy just as she was alive from achieving praise.

"Did you like my song?" she asked joyfully.

"I did. It was clever as it was humorous. And need I say, catchy. Do you write songs often?"

"As much as I can. I just wish I could get paid for doing so."

"That, little lady, is a dream worth chasing," he assured.

"Not sure how. No one wants to pay to listen to the songs *I* write."

"That's not true, not from what I just witnessed. However, you might be better off somewhere that serves more than month-old swish. Just a thought. Take care Kara." He made his way past her.

"Where you staying tonight?" she asked.

"I usually camp, but I may ask the barkeep if he has an extra room."

"I'm sure he does. I'll ask. Take care, mister, and thanks for the advice."

"No, thank you for the show. It alone was worth my travels."

Marx opened the door and invited the smokeless air into his lungs. Although the stables influenced the smell, the crisp air was preferred. Rearing around the stables, he heard a man's voice from the other side.

"Give me that!"

"Let go!" a woman's voice screamed.

"I will and be gone once you hand it over. Not until then."

Two fingers pressed behind the man's collarbone.

"I'll make this very easy. Leave at once," Marx stated calmly.

The man went to turn, but as he did, Marx pressed down—hard, forcing him to his knees.

"Ma'am, do you mind moving?" Marx asked.

The lady moved as Marx used the bottom of his boot to kick the thief facedown into a convenient pile of horse manure. Enraged, he turned to find a drawn blade at his throat. The stable's lantern gave Marx the details he needed to know the man if he decided to take vengeance.

"Now, will you leave?" Marx asked.

The man's dung-covered face scowled. Marx waited for the answer.

"Yeah, I'll leave," he said.

"We appreciate it." Marx lowered his blade and stepped to the side. The man ran off.

"Are you okay?" Marx asked.

"I'm fine. Thank you …"

"Marx, may I ask your name?" Marx asked.

The dim light showed her hesitance.

"You don't have to give it. However, I am curious. What brings you way out here?"

"Business, but I can't find who I'm looking for."

"Care to describe him for me?"

"He's not from around here, that's for sure. It's okay, I'll be headed back to the harbor. Thank you, again." Her eyes and lips glistened. The spell broke when she whipped her hair, turning toward the stables to retrieve her horse.

"You think it's safe riding back alone at this hour?" Marx asked.

"I'll be fine. I was without my bow. Thank you once again, Marx.

"Sorry girl. You won't be resting as I assured you would. Double cups of oats when we get back to Laneloon." She let the beast's nose nestle in her palm.

The horse snorted with a flap of her lips and a whip of her tail.

Marx made his way into the stable as the lady disappeared into the black blanket of night. He looked up into the stars. "Watch out for her, will you?"

Believing that his prayer was heard, he spent the next few minutes talking to his own horse. While he talked with his riding companion, the blood of those inside was thinning, as were their judgements.

"Rifi! You cheated!" Kara accused.

The lily elf was taken aback. "Did not!"

"Many more card cards," the goblin strung together words that agreed with Kara

"Kagu, I do not. See," Rifi showed the back of his cards.

"Me thinked more," Kagu replied, his black beady eyes lost in confusion.

"It's okay buddy," Rifi said.

"Let's see inside ye pockets," the dwarf suggested.

"Whärnook, are you serious?' Rifi asked.

"I got twenty reds at stake, and I already lost twelve," Whärnook claimed.

"Fine. Be my guest," Rifi took off his jacket to let Kara search. "The nerve," he added.

Kara did a thorough search before handing it back.

"Sorry Rifi." Kara sighed, "Looks like you win then."

"Apology accepted. From *you*, Kara, I don't recall getting one from Whärnook," Rifi said stiffly.

"Aye, when I'm wrong, I'm wrong. And so, I'm done fer the night." Whärnook returned as he got up, letting go of what he lost.

Noticing that Kagu was picking at something under the table, Ethen tried to signal Kagu to stop. Kara, picking up on this, distracted Whärnook.

"I hear ya. I hope luck finds its way back to you *and* me. I'm out too. Ethen, you ready?" Kara signaled Rifi, hoping he would stop Kagu when it was too late.

Kagu lifted a card, found stuck underneath the table. Whärnook gave one last glance.

"Where'd that come from?" Whärnook asked.

"Kagu, you cheated!" Rifi accused.

"Kagu, that's not okay," Kara said.

"Me no cheat. Founded low low table." Kagu pointed underneath the table.

"He lost a long time ago. Why would *he* cheat?" Whärnook pointed out. "That explains everything. Rifi, ye cheated fer the last time."

Whärnook got up and reached for Rifi's collar. Rifi evaded, quickly leaping out of his seat.

"You can't prove that I did anything," he said as he escaped from the corner. "Kara, can you collect my winnings for me? I'll be going now."

Whärnook's bushy eyebrows furrowed, the sign all dwarves give when ready to fight.

"Ye aren't going anywhere, ya little scamp," Whärnook roared, flinging his chair like a piece of kindling, unknowingly hitting someone.

"Calm down. We don't know Kagu didn't find that card there himself. Who knows what goes on inside a goblin's head?" Kara said.

"Don't defend him, lass. We all might not know what goes on inside a goblin's head, but we sure know they're too stupid to stash cards. Especially when he wer out five games ago." Whärnook stomped toward Rifi.

"Who threw this chair?" A tall, muscular man, in his late fifties, reached for his sword. A red insignia stripped across the Mother's Crest embedded in his armor showed he was a retired war veteran.

"Ye the cause of this baby elf. This ain't over," Whärnook shifted his attention, and rage, toward the retired warrior. It is well known that once a dwarf reaches a certain level of anger, they tend to keep it for a while. "It was an accident. Now, lower ye sword, old man, before I make ya eat it."

"Me no stupid!" Kagu screeched as he lunged toward Whärnook, landing on his back while pulling on his beard from behind.

"Mindless gutter trash!" Whärnook roared as he frantically used his stubby arms, trying to grab the goblin.

"Me no mutter trash too," Kagu yelled.

The veteran laughed as he sat back down. "Suits you right, stumpy."

Kagu crawled around until Whärnook grabbed hold of one of his legs. With a yank, he detached the goblin and flung him across the tavern, who landed on the same old veteran.

"What the? That's it, you short stack of troll excrement." The old man pulled his sword free.

Whärnook reached for his axe. "I'll make it quick, geezer."

Confused, Kagu's eyes darted around and landed on the man towering over him, sword in hand. Seeing this new threat up close, the goblin snarled, baring his razor-sharp teeth.

Kara rushed to intervene. "Everyone calm down. Whärnook, you can have all your money back. Here it is." She held out a handful of coins before facing the vet. "Sir, please don't kill him. He's not your average goblin."

"The only good goblin is a dead one," the man replied.

"He's just scared, is all," Kara urged.

Ethen joined her, with his wooden sword in hand. Rifi rounded the tables.

"Out of my way, street hussy," the old man said.

"Take that back," Ethen demanded as he stepped forward.

"Ethen! No!" Kara went to grab him, but he was too quick.

"Boy, I can't take back the truth," the man snickered.

"Kagu, attack!" Ethen was ready to swing when the man was preoccupied with a ferocious goblin.

Kagu sprung toward the vet's face as quick and high as a cricket. An elbow threw, smashing Kagu's jaw. The strike was precise and forceful, knocking the goblin unconscious. Ethen didn't find the distraction he was hoping for. Still, he edged toward the experienced warrior. His eyes found Rifi, daggers drawn, sneaking up behind the man. He hoped, once again, he could catch the vet off guard. The veteran caught Ethen's gaze and spun, kicking Rifi in the chest. Ethen swung. The vet turned back just in time to block.

"A wooden sword? Ha!" the man mocked and swung hard enough to chip away at Ethen's sword. Two more swings and the wooden sword broke in half. "Time to teach the young a lesson. A price you'll pay with that hand you struck me with."

"Ethen!" Kara screamed as the man raised his sword.

Kara was shoved out of the way. Whärnook's speed took the vet by surprise. The charging dwarf aimed for the vet's stomach, using his head as a battering ram. The charge lifted and carried the man through tables, chairs and any persons that were in the way. The veteran tried to recover as Whärnook jumped, lifting his stout body as high he could, before bringing down his club-like fist. The vet failed. Whärnook swapped hands, not losing a beat. The first few punches thudded loudly, silencing everyone and their drunk conversations. The thuds gave way to splintering cracks.

"Dwarf! Get off him!" Vonnie pointed a crossbow at Whärnook's head. "Last thing I need is another investigation. Is he dead?"

Whärnook looked down at a caved-in face. "Aye, he be choppin' no wee-lad's limbs off. That's fer true."

"Oh, that's just great! He was once part of Queen Cillian's army. Well-known too. Some even say a hero. Well, that's it everyone, fun's over. Hullbert grab a few men and shovels. I'm sure Whärnook will be glad to help." Vonnie raised his eyebrow. "Well?"

"Sorry bout that Vonnie. Sure, I'll help," Whärnook said shamefully.

"And what about my furniture?"

Kara walked up with a handful of coins, "This ought about cover the mess and the trouble."

Folks joined as the body disappeared out the back entrance.

The entrance swung open as Marx entered. The eyes in the tavern shifted around and away, the voices unusually low.

Vonnie tucked his crossbow behind the bar, turned, and faced Marx. "Kara said you're interested in a room. We just had one open."

Chapter Two

Blame it on the Swish

The angle of the blade allowed Marx to feel each rib as he leaned all of his weight in. His foe shook until the last breath left. The head shifted as the last effort to live was no more. The dead eyes landed on Marx as if to congratulate him. Looking around, he noticed all the eyes of those he'd killed were on him. This surrounding place echoed what the rest of the world felt like—alone. He was now the only one left to roam the world, or so it seemed. He couldn't recall why he was fighting. His bloodlust still pumped in his forearms, the very muscles that controlled his blade, and ran into his heart. The carnage didn't dampen his ecstasy.

Moment caught his eye. His blade rose and after a glance, lowered. It was a woman in a yellow dress. Her beauty was beyond comparison. She looked familiar although he couldn't place her. She looked down at the bodies. He wished he could have hidden them, or thrown his blade to the side, but he couldn't shield her from the obvious truth. Gauging her reaction, he waited for fear or disgrace, but neither came. Rather, pity.

The morning sun lit up Marx's room with a bright glow. Thanks to the late drinkers, he didn't get the full night's sleep he'd hoped for. Still, he found time to meditate and pray until the drunkards drank themselves into silence. Now it seemed the bird's turn to make a racket. Fighting from the morning's sleep, he stared out the window as his mind's wheels turned slowly.

He chased after his fleeting dream. Catching glimpses, he saw the woman he saved the night before. Thankful it wasn't real, he turned on his other side, away from the light. From his dog who passed, and his last assignment complete, he knew the last chapter in his life had closed. He had half a mind to travel northeast but being so close to the harbor, at the very least, there was an old friend to visit and a plate of the harbor's delicious lemon steamed mussels to devour.

His thoughts veered to the siblings, Kara, and Ethen. Kara was extremely talented, while Ethen was looking to become a swordsman. Both were young and determined to become something much more. Kara had made a good point in their disagreement, that they could very well die on the battlefield; death is a necessity in any war. The tension Marx felt since the storm loomed over him like an unseen ghost. It warned that the young, especially ones so spirited, should never invite death so early. He figured if those two were going to Laneloon Harbor and fate threw them back his way, he'd do his part to extend a hand. It'd be up to them to grab hold of it.

As his thoughts returned to the lady in the yellow dress and a sudden craving for lemon steamed mussels, his mind was made up. He sat up. A nomad's story never starts; rather the pages just continue to turn. If he left now he could make it there by noon. He collected his things, kneeled, and whispered a soft prayer for safe travels and wise discernment.

Making his way back into the bar, bodies lay over tables and on the floor. The barrel that gave the tavern its name was knocked over, empty. Scanning, he saw Ethen lying next to his sister in the corner.

His tracker skills kicked in when he saw traces of blood marks, hinting of a dragged body toward the back door. Heavy clumps of dried mud matched the pair of boots of a fellow sleeping under a table. A pair of muddy shovels behind the bar, along with the murmurs when he reentered last night, strengthened his suspicion of what had happened. *A regular occasion in a place like this*, Marx assumed, as he put the thought out of his mind.

Stepping outside, he was happy to bid the smell of The Hairy Barrel farewell, once and for all. He came up behind his horse that was happy to see his rider.

"Ages, old boy, how'd you sleep?" Marx asked, rubbing the horse's nose. "Ready to see Laneloon harbor? The first harbor those traveling from the north see in over a week, even after seeing land all that time. You see, the entire northern strait is comprised of cliffs, too steep to dock. So, the sailors are teased before finally arriving at the harbor. It has been some time since I visited.

"Well, how about it, boy? You ready?" Marx saddled up and jumped on Ages' back. "Then let's get."

Marx left the lonely tavern and rode the only road west that led to the harbor. It was nice to see the sun come out to dry up the land. The scattered puddles were reminders that the rain conquered the last few days. With the wound of his late canine still sore, the sun reminded him that life intended to move along, leaving the past behind where it belonged. Still, he wished he could turn sideways to scratch his old pup behind his ear. The sting kept him focused on Ages' tempo to reach their destination before the sun hung directly above him. He kept his pace strong until a voice shouted off the beaten path.

"Is anyone there? My mum—she's dead!" the voice yelled, a child's voice.

Marx jumped off his horse, slipped off his necklace, and wrapped it around his hand before grabbing his hilt. He reared around a thicket. A large man, belly fat pouring out of his armor, continued yelling. Marx's eyes darted, spotting armed men around him and shifting in the branches above. Marx continued forward.

"I don't know what to do. Please help me…" the fat man stopped at the sight of Marx.

"That's pretty good," Marx admitted. "Can you do any other impersonations?"

The fat man chuckled, trading his high-pitched tone for a deeper one. "How 'bout a sucker who fell for an ambush?"

"Hmm, haven't heard that one before. How's it go?" Marx kept notice of the bowmen behind trees and bushes—all pointing their notched arrows at him.

"Let me show you." The fat man picked up the large club leaning against him. "Resist and you die. We just want the necklace."

"How'd you know about that?" Marx asked.

"We been on you for a bit now. You've had a good dash, now give it here. Those boys up there can split an apple from double the distance they're at. You don't have to die today."

"Although I don't have to die today, I do have to die *some*day. Funny how our warped perspective of time drives us to make decisions we ought not to. Forgetting time is equal to nothing when eternity is possible."

"Beautifully said, *poet*. Now drop your blade or *time* will no longer be a factor," the fat man raised his club.

Marx lowered his head and gripped his handle.

* * * * *

Kara forced her eyes open. Her head heavy, she dragged herself to a nearby window. *Fourth hour*, she noticed. Thinking what today had planned for her, she grumbled. In no way did she want to join any army, especially one she didn't feel at all passionate about. Still, she wanted to go to Laneloon Harbor. It was always a treat to see the different kinds of people come together to trade. Her favorite were ones with fancy clothes paired with the lack of wit. She saw her brother still sleeping and decided against waking him up. Although she was partly inclined to check out the recruitment tent, she figured she would prolong the journey, slimming the chances of joining.

Standing up, her head screeched. She rubbed her temples to ease the thumping and once her brain recovered, daily schemes for survival started laying their foundation. *Well*, she thought, *if Ethen and I join the military, we'd less likely be coming back here anytime soon.* She wondered if Vonnie would trust her enough to take his carriage to the harbor. She recalled him saying something about needing supplies and how he hates to travel at his age. Too bad to find out that his carriage, and any money he might give for supplies, never made it back.

She looked around the tavern and saw Rifi lying next to Whärnook. The last she remembered, Whärnook was about to tear Rifi's head off his shoulders. Then the memory of the retired veteran came to mind, mainly his corpse dragged out the backdoor. *Did that really happen?* she asked herself, searching her memory for more. Blurry images surfaced: Rifi getting a hold of Vonnie's crossbow and pointing it at Whärnook, a rogue bolt nearly missing Hallbert's hand and the three laughing with their arms slung around each other.

It's probably a good idea to say goodbye to the swish too, she told herself. She dragged herself to the bar where a bowl of water was left out.

"Uhh, Kara?" Ethen mumbled as he sat up. "I don't feel good."

"That makes two of us," she replied, as she gulped down a handful of water. "We can always try again tomorrow."

"What time is it?" Ethen shot up to gauge the sun. "We gotta go. We can still make it."

Kara cursed herself. She almost protested but grew fond of the thought: leaving this place for good. She had plenty of ways to get out of recruitment from here to the harbor.

"Very well, brother. A deal's a deal." Kara raised her eyebrow slightly and shot Ethen a smirk only he knew. "I wanted to see if Vonnie might need some help getting anything at Laneloon."

Ethen's stomach turned. He nodded reluctantly.

"That's very kind of you, Kara," Vonnie said as he came through the doorway from behind the bar. "I could use the help. I need to stay here anyway as that stoop Whärnook created a potential pain in my arse."

Kara wasn't sure if he was baiting or not.

"We just wanted enough to get something to eat at Laneloon, if that's okay." She studied his reaction.

"I suppose that's fair. Nothing too fancy. How's eight reds sound?"

"Sounds good to me." She turned to Ethen with the same raised eyebrow.

"Hallbert," Vonnie yelled.

"Hallbert?"

"Sure, I need to send someone to make sure you won't run off with my carriage and coin."

"You don't trust me?" She played offended.

"I'm gonna miss ya, Kara. Don't get killed too early after recruitment."

"You knew?"

"Can't swindle a scoundrel."

"Look, part of the reason we're leaving is we're tired of lying and stealing to live." She looked up at Vonnie. "You mad?"

"Nah. If you got away from stealing from *me*, I'd blame myself. You know my code and my view; possessions are temporary. But you lied to me again. You're not tired of lying and stealing." He tilted his head toward Ethen. "He is. He's a wise and ambitious boy. You'd be dim not to pay him heed."

Nearing seven foot tall, Hallbert rounded the corner in his sleep attire that didn't pair with his grungy self. Bright yellow silk with dark-blue star patches stitched in loose pajamas appeared comfy*, and that they belonged to a well-off commoner.* His thick red beard ended in whips, which mimicked his hair, flying in all directions. His daunting stare with sunken eyes waited for others to notice them and assume the worst. His skin showed off its years of dirt and grime that won the war against the few days of river baths. Each thick finger held a long yellow fingernail, some that he used to scratch his hairy underbelly as he stopped mid step to finish his yawn.

"What is it?" he asked.

"We need supplies. I have a list, and we need to check that our dear late friend doesn't have others who might come looking for him, but for the gods' sake, go get dressed first. You look like an overgrown, hairy five-year-old." Vonnie shooed him away.

Hallbert looked down as if forgetting what he was wearing. Catching the comment, he shrugged and walked off.

"Uhhh," a deep moan, louder than most mortals, came from the stirring dwarf by the fireplace.

"Get up Whärnook! You owe me more than what Kara was nice enough to pay last night. I have a mission for you," Vonnie yelled.

Whärnook stood up. "After serving that poison and making *us* pay fer it, I think ye owe me."

Vonnie eyed the dwarf as he approached the bar.

"Aye, just a joke. Keep yer boots on. I understand the position I put ye in." Whärnook grabbed the bowl of water and drank it down to its last drop, expelling a loud and long "*aaah.*" "What would ye have me do?"

"Follow me." Vonnie tilted his head toward the back of the bar.

"Oh no! My sword, I forgot that old scum…" Ethen remembered what had happened to the dead veteran—he quickly blamed the swish instead.

"Oh boy, do I feel like a floppy fish. What was in that barrel?" Rifi moaned as he looked around. "Where's Kagu?"

"I don't know," Ethen replied. "Kara, you seen Kagu?"

"Nope."

"That green death trap." Rifi made his way around the bar, yelling Kagu's name, leading him outside.

"It looks like Vonnie's gonna buy us one last meal and a free ride to Laneloon. Eh, Whärnook drank all the water. Here, let's get you some water." Kara grabbed the bowl and led the way outside.

The sunlight brought the thumping back into their skulls.

"I can't believe I let you talk me into drinking that pee," Ethen said.

"I'm told it will put hair on that chest of yours," Kara replied.

"I'd rather be rid of this headache."

The two approached the well spout.

"Kagu….Kagu…" Rifi continued yelling.

After Ethen got his fill of water, he too became concerned for their goblin friend.

"You think he's okay?" Ethen asked.

"Not sure. There's a reason no one knows how long goblins live, naturally that is. They all die well beforehand. *Kagu!*" Kara joined.

None saw Kagu tilting on the edge of the stable-roof behind them. Still sleeping, he rolled over and fell.

THUMP

They turned to see Kagu get up, utterly confused. Looking at Ethen and Kara, he smiled with blood smeared around his mouth.

"Kar Kar, Ethone. Sun high soon wake," Kagu said, pointing at the sun overhead.

"Yes, you slept in. We all did," Ethen said. "Are you okay? Where did that blood come from?"

"Dark skies bites. Find bush bush tails," Kagu explained.

Ethen looked over to Rifi to see what was said.

"He went to find a midnight snack and found a squirrel. Right?"

Kagu only stared back, giving no indication of the answer.

"Anyway, where were you? Didn't you hear me yelling your name?" Rifi checked his companion.

"Sky?" Kagu replied with a blank stare, hoping he found the correct answer.

"Just glad you're okay," Rifi said. "Speaking of, how's that jaw?"

"Jaw still jaw."

"That's good."

Vonnie, Whärnook, and Hallbert came out of the tavern, Hallbert wearing his more appropriate leather armor.

"Hallbert, get the coach ready," Vonnie said, approaching Kara and Ethen.

"You two be careful out there. You'll soon discover that those who desire war are much less honorable than thieves. They easily trade lives for personal gain and then have the gall to call *themselves* the heroes. Stay sharp." Vonnie threw Kara a small sack.

From the sound and weight, it felt like a good bit of coin. She opened the sack to confirm what was inside. "Vonnie, you don't have to give me *this* much. After I tried to steal from you?"

"That was the entertainment from last night. You're welcome," Vonnie said with a smile that lasted a second before he grunted and turned around. "Now get out of here, you little heaps."

"Thank you!" Kara yelled before he walked up to The Hairy Barrel, glanced one more time, and shut the door behind him. She looked at the sack, the first payment she got for one of her songs. She gripped the purse, thinking what the stranger, Marx had said.

Whärnook laughed with Rifi. "To think how sore I got that ye cheated me. Little did ye know, I cheated the second game in."

"Pfft. I knew the whole time. I had bigger plans to get it all back with interest," Rifi returned. "If it wasn't for Kagu, I'd be sitting pretty."

They shared a laugh as Kagu joined in, unaware of what he was laughing at. Whärnook continued. "I could swear there was something off about that brew last night. I really lost it there."

"So, you think we could catch a ride with you to Laneloon?" Rifi asked Kara.

"It's not up to me, but I don't see why not. Hallbert's a big softy. Wait, how can Kagu go?" Kara asked.

"We just strap some shackles on him, and *kapoof,* he's my prisoner. We might even sell him for some coin." Rifi's chuckle disappeared at Kagu's growl.

Hallbert came around with a two-horse carriage and stopped in front of the five.

"You coming with?" Rifi asked Whärnook.

"Nye. I'm headed to Falonship. On me way, I have rumors to spread and a mission to fake. Again, I wasn't thinking straight last night." He turned to Kara. "Fine singing lass and thanks for teaching me the words. I'll sing it every tavern I come across." Whärnook looked at Ethen. "I heard ye want to join the army. It ain't so bad. Pay is pay and ye two aren't as dimwitted as most. Ye may end up leading those empty skulls or rob em all blind. Either way, ye'll fare just fine." He turned to address everyone. "I'll be goin now. Take care ye good fer nothings."

"See ya. I'll find another way to get that coin of yours." Rifi said.

"I bet ye will, baby elf." Whärnook snickered.

"You mind if we catch a ride?" Rifi asked Hallbert.

"Join or jump off a cliff, I don't care which," he answered.

"I think we'll join."

The carriage went left as Whärnook went right, humming and mumbling Kara's tune.

"…because the bad got nothin' better to do."

* * * * *

The carriage kept steady as everyone onboard soaked in the silence to keep their hangovers at bay. Rifi and Kagu's larger ears perked.

"Kiddy kid cries," Kagu said.

"I hear it too," Rifi confirmed.

"Hear what?" Ethen asked.

"Some kid, he's crying for help."

The others heard as well when they got closer.

"Stop the carriage," Kara said.

Hallbert stopped and shared a look to check it out. They jumped off and continued cautiously. Hallbert gripped his longsword, Rifi held his twin knives, Kagu bared his teeth, while Ethen, missing his wooden sword, held out his pocket blade. Kara stepped in front.

"It's just a kid. Calm down, will ya?"

"It seems you've never been ambushed or set an ambush before. Just stay behind me," Hallbert whispered as he led, surprisingly quietly for a large man.

Turning around a large thicket, he saw several men tied up against a large tree with arrows lodged throughout the surroundings. An extra-large fellow spoke in a child's voice. Giving the area one last look, he lowered his weapon and came out. The man switched to his normal, lower voice.

"Oh, thank the gods. Sorry, I was faking. I just wasn't sure anyone would come help us. Please quick, free us, will ya?"

Kara and the rest came from behind.

"There's no kid," Hallbert confirmed.

"Like I said, I'm sorry. I didn't think anyone would come. That was a voice I do for my daughter." He chuckled slightly. "Pretty good, huh?"

"Boy, is he a terrible liar," Rifi said.

"Liar? Why do you say that?" The man asked, shifting his glance to Kagu's dead stare and dried blood around his mouth.

"Well, for starters, your eyes shift three times too many, your breathing is irregular, and your voice is high, and I'm not talking about the charade you pulled. Which, I will admit, ain't half bad," Rifi said.

"Rifi here is a bit of a lie reader. So, we're gonna start with three simple questions and see how you do. Who are you? What are you doing out here? And why are you tied up?" Hallbert got comfortable, leaning up against a tree.

"We're mercenaries—"

"Sorry to interrupt you so early," Hallbert said. "But I feel it's necessary to give you a fair warning. I saw you notice our unusual friend there." He pointed at Kagu. "Not sure how much you know about goblins. I'd bet you know that they fight to the death and because of their much smaller size, don't last long. However, you're in no position to defend yourself, and goblins enjoy their meals to squirm while they eat. Do you catch my meaning?"

"He means he won't kill you as he eats you. If he can help it, that is," Rifi answered.

"That was my meaning, yes. Thank you, Todd," Hallbert said. "Now, this saves me the trouble of dealing with you, if you *are* lying that is, while feeding my friend here at the same time. Two birds and all. Understand, as far as the law goes, this ill fate of yours is not necessarily murder. All I'm doing is not stopping him from eating you, which could be viewed as simply not putting myself in harm's way. Extremely hard to prove otherwise. If your lot is something special, that is. Do we understand each other?"

Giving Kagu one last look who licked his lips, the man began.

"We *are,* in fact, mercenaries, but we're not after any person but an item. There is a man who came from the tavern east of here who carries it. We lured him right where that boy stands now." He nodded to Ethen. "He was the target we were told has the item."

"What's he look like?" Hallbert asked.

"Black hair, tan skin, handsome. He wore a cloak that had been well traveled."

Kara and Hallbert shared a look.

"So, you've seen him?" the man asked.

"I'll be asking the questions," Hallbert said sternly. "So, how is it you failed to acquire this item?"

The man paused, not sure how to respond.

"Well?" Hallbert pressed.

Sighing, he continued. "He was faster than anything known. The arrows you noticed were evaded as soon as they were shot. Each time he slowed back down, we'd try again. I swung my club wide with as much strength and speed as I could and he just let me. He was toying with us. When we were out of breath, he told us he would tie us to this tree.

"We tried to stop him, but he easily ignored our attempts to fend him off as a parent would a stubborn toddler. Again, he was faster than anything known." The man's eyes looked up at Hallbert. "I swear it."

"He's telling the truth," Rifi confirmed. "Or at least he thinks he is."

"Is that so?" Hallbert said, amused. "What do you think possessed this man to achieve such a feat?"

"He was either a witch or a wizard," the man replied.

"Not likely, as each of those, or at least as powerful as you say, no longer exists." Hallbert got up from leaning.

"We know what we saw, and I can't imagine anything else," the man protested.

Hallbert kneeled to eye the man more closely. "Tell me more about this item."

The man's gaze shifted back to Kagu as if to ask if it was worth it.

"Trust me fella, I'm not good at bluffing because I never do. Part of the reason I never play cards." Hallbert leaned over, blocking the man's view of Kagu. "I just asked you a question."

"Will you let us go?" the man asked.

"I will if you answer me."

The man sighed. "A pendant, a necklace. An intricate molding of five vines, with tiny leaves sprouting off. They come together in the center, like a knot of five pieces of rope."

"Hmm. Did you ever stop and think that it was the necklace that gave this man his powers? An item like that, as rare as it might be, *does* exist. It woulda been wise to acquire the necklace a bit more cautiously." Hallbert looked back at his friends. "Well, this was quite the start to the new day."

"You gonna free us?"

Hallbert laughed. "Not before I rob you blind. Those weapons of yours aren't cheap and that armor—"

"You son of a shite-soaked pig!" the man yelled.

"No need for name calling, as accurate as that claim might be. Now, I *was* gonna free ya, naked and defenseless, but bringing my moms into this crossed some sort of polite line, I'm sure." Hallbert turned back to his company. "You guys wanna make some coin? I need help stripping these fellas bare."

Chapter Three

Let Down but Fried Food

Laneloon Harbor was unusually busy as the sun revisited their streets. During the storm, merchants lost opportunities while townsfolk got bored, caged inside their houses. They were now free to take in the rays, flood the streets, and sail on the sea. Children ran a little further, voices rose a little higher, and fishermen reeled in a little faster. Shoppers spent a little more while shopkeepers were happy to accommodate. The central park acted as the harbor's wheel, the streets its spokes, each fanning out, providing shops on every stretch.

A local band came to meet the crowds. Each member mastered a rare instrument, each found from a different corner of the world. The Fishy School was woven together over the years by their love of music. They filled the town with their catchy and unique tune that danced all the way to the docks.

This was just one touch many found enchanting about Laneloon.

What others adored was the food. Thanks to the northern strait, a variety of trades and recipes had sailed in often—the halflings' herbs, the hill dwarves' craft of smoked meat, and the elf-inspired delectable dishes. Combined with unified humans of Tannonfalle and their coastal taste for seafood, the harbor had discovered dishes not found anywhere else.

The unique trait of Laneloon—all foreigners, despite race, were granted access to trade and rest in its inns, aside from o'rüks, o'gürs, and goblins. As long as they kept the peace and stayed inside the town's borders, they could visit. Some questioned whether this was Queen Cillian's way of inviting peace, or a way for her to tax the other races, even those considered enemies.

The truth was Laneloon had created its own laws. They didn't bother receiving aid from the queen or any of the five kingdoms like every other town or city on the continent of Tannonfalle. The harbor contributed more than enough for taxes while affording their own small army. It had found the balance between generously supporting its neighbors while suggesting a hassle not to interfere with their ways. All in all, peace was seen in the streets and the queen's army was always welcomed. Although enemies met here in plain sight, both powerless to overcome the other, Laneloon birthed a new law. A law that brought with it a new kind of corruption. A law put simply, that here, coin is king.

Marx passed through the city gate after showing his papers. He was surprised at how many folk crowded the roads of what was once a small harbor. Laneloon doubled since the last time he visited. A few new buildings and attractions caught his eye as children ran past him. A funny thought came to him, these kids and those buildings didn't exist the last time he walked this same road. Scanning the different shops, some known and some new, his eyes rested when he found the only building that didn't change one bit.

He added a harmonized bob of the head as he walked, hearing a catchy tune across the street. A nearby hitch provided more than enough room to tie off his horse. He was pleasantly surprised to see a trough, offering his horse a drink while he waited.

"Would you look at that? Here you go, old boy. You mind waiting while I go grab a bite to eat?" Marx tied Ages down as his stomach grumbled at the sniff of delicious meats: barbecued, baked, smoked, and fried.

Across the street stood his destination, the Squirming Squid. Opening the door, everything looked the same aside from the furniture and unknown faces. A young woman at the front smiled as he entered.

"Hello, Sir. Is it just you today?" she asked.

"It is. Thank you," he answered.

She led him to a small table by the front window.

"Would you like me to fetch you a menu?"

"Menu?"

"It has the items listed of what we serve here."

"You still serve lemon steamed mussels and fried squid?" Marx asked.

"We sure do."

"I'll have both. I have some catching up to do."

"I'll have that up as soon as possible." As she turned, Marx stopped her.

"Excuse me, miss. Does Pete still run this place?"

"I'm sorry, Sir, I'm not sure who that is."

"Who owns this diner?"

"Eddy. I think he is still here. Would you like to speak with him?"

Eddy, Marx thought. He was nearly ten the last time he visited. To think that would make him in his mid-twenties now, around the age Marx was then.

"Wow, time *does* fly." He spoke to himself, admiring the youth found in the hostess.

"Excuse me, Sir?"

"Sorry, miss. I was just speaking of time; it moves fast enough to get away from you. Yes, please. Tell him an old friend of his dad would like to say hi."

"I'll go check to see if he's still here and put in this order. Just a moment,"

Looking out the window, he took in the activity outside. He didn't stare long. A young man with short brown hair, freckles and dark eyes approached him.

"Hello Sir, may I help you?"

"Eddy? Is that you?" Marx stood up to eye him closely. "It is you. I'm an old friend of your dad's. You remember me? My name is Marx. I, too, looked much younger when we last met. Oh, about fourteen or fifteen years ago, I'd say. I taught you the dice game Dead Kraken."

"I've taught a load of customers that game over the years." Eddy's cheery demeanor stiffened. "I'm sorry to say, my father is no longer with us. He passed away two winters ago. He had a stomach disease that lasted a year before it finally claimed him." The young man's sadness turned peaceful. "I'm almost not sorry he finally passed. At least now he is free from the pain."

Marx put his hand on Eddy's shoulder. "You have grown to become quite wise. Yes, I believe he is in a much better place. I'm going to miss him. He was the best cook there was, and I've never met a funnier man."

The two shared a smile at the thought of some of Pete's crude jokes.

"It doesn't look like you're doing too bad. I've never seen so many people in here and by the smell of it, he taught you the tricks of the trade," Marx said.

"He did, and I added a few of my own specialties to the menu. I must recommend *Pete's Demise*. It's a spicy dish I concocted. It's a local favorite."

"Pete's demise? It looks like you also gained his sick sense of humor," Marx laughed.

"I was about to leave but would love to catch up with one of my father's old friends. That is, if you got some good stories to tell. Perhaps of you two getting into trouble?"

"I think I got you covered," Marx pulled out a chair and got ready to tell a story that Eddy was now old enough to hear.

Hallbert's papers were handed back. The guard advised Hallbert that his cell would be kept warm for him, an ongoing jest that had lasted years. Rifi was told to keep Kagu shackled. Rifi convinced the guard he would do just that while holding a knife at his green friend's throat. The carriage stopped in front of a large barn on the outskirts of town.

The barn was not open to the public but to those who were part of the underground trading world most referred to as the Thieves' Trade. However, those involved didn't like the name because they didn't like any title that would identify them with those who got caught. The Trade's code was simple: no stealing from the less fortunate and no talking to the authorities while keeping your fellow thief out of trouble if possible. The view was shared—it is better to work within the constraints of the Trade than in shackles and jail cells. One way they'd achieve this was by using their own language. Vocal communication was an obvious way to get found out. Rather, they used slight hand and facial gestures that communicated enough to conduct business, warn others, and barter. This kept trading illegal items out of the ears of those trying to accumulate enough evidence for an arrest.

By paying a percentage to the Thieves' Trade and keeping their mouths shut, they were granted privileges. They had access to fences and secret shop locations of the stolen wares and sometimes, were even bailed out of jail. This privilege spread to the other major cities as certain thieves became known contributors to the cause and treated as such.

Those who weren't friends among the Trade had a hard time getting by with living a criminal's life. Some of the thief tax funded sketch artists and reporters to draw or write a summary, detailing enemies, or those who caused risks. This way, they could alert members and even the authorities to take necessary action to keep the business afloat.

Hallbert pulled back on the reins as the carriage halted. The rest on board jumped off and stretched their legs.

"Wait out here. I'll be back with your coin." Hallbert signaled to a fellow who opened the barn doors before the carriage disappeared inside.

Twenty or so minutes later, Hallbert came back out and tossed Rifi and Kara each a sack of coin.

"I think you'll find that fair," Hallbert said.

"I think you and I have a different meaning of fair," Rifi replied.

"Oh? How is it you'd manage getting your share here in the first place?" Hallbert raised his pinkie twice while tilting his arm slightly to the right.

Rifi scratched behind his left ear while raising his upper lip. The rest of the silent conversation consisted of other stares and gestures that ultimately resulted in Rifi admitting it was fair enough.

"So, you're off to join Cillian's army," Hallbert said to Kara and Ethen. "Good luck. I've always wondered what my life would look like if I joined myself. I could be some sergeant or maybe retired by now."

"Or dead," Rifi said.

"Or dead," Hallbert agreed with a chuckle that stopped when he saw Kara's concern. "Not that you should be worried. Whärnook was right. You'll be just fine, I'm sure. Either way, it was good knowing you two. If you're ever in the area, stop by. Unless you're there to arrest me." Hallbert turned to Rifi and Kagu. "What about you two?"

"I'm going to make my rounds around town. Meet up at The Gist?" Rifi said.

"Sure, I'll be staying there tonight. I have no want to run into that naked lot of sour men tonight. See you there." Hallbert snapped the reins.

"Kara, Ethen, I'd be lying to say I won't miss you two. But as Hallbert suggested, this life isn't as rewarding as it's cracked up to be. Just keep your wits about you. Bring it in," Rifi said as he went in for a hug that was met with a handshake.

"I'll be better off with my property still with me, thanks," Kara said.

"There's that wit I was talking about. Ethen?" Rifi extended his hand as Ethen accepted and shook it.

Kagu, confused, didn't know what was going on until this point.

"You go forever gone?" Kagu said sadly.

"Yes Kagu. We have a chance to live a better life than this." Ethen laid out his hand for a handshake.

"You are a very special goblin. Proof that looks aren't everything," Kara finished.

Kagu's black eyes glossed over.

"Me no forever gone!" Kagu yelled as he tried to fling his chained hands around the siblings.

"There, there. Not forever gone. Just a little while gone," Kara said softly as she patted his back.

"We'll be back," Ethen lied.

"Yeah, buddy. They'll be back in no time. Come on Kagu, let's go get some bites. Farewell you two," Rifi said as he pushed Kagu in the other direction.

"Come on Kara. Recruitment tent is this way," Ethen said.

Kara followed as she recounted the two sacks of coin she received that day.

"You know, we have enough here for both of us to live like kings for at least a week. Live like we usually do for over a month." Kara said, dropping coins as she counted a second time.

"After that, then what? We steal some more? We lie to more of our friends? Or we get someone else killed? *Or* we save it. Maybe buy a small home in the east?" Ethen kept his pace.

Kara didn't want to admit he had a point and so she kept her mouth closed. A breeze brought with it the tasty scents of the harbor. Ethen interjected her thoughts.

"Let's just go check out the tent, ask some questions and we'll get something to eat. It's right here," he said.

"Fine."

The tent had a short line of two young men waiting to talk to the recruitment officers. Each was given time to ask questions and get answers about pay, requirements, and duties. All sounded reasonably fair. Kara's nervous hands clenched as the thought of joining the army was becoming a reality far too fast. She forced her brain, that had run out of excuses, not to give up. *There has to be a way out*, she thought. With fair pay, free housing, free training, *and* travel, she knew talking Ethen out of this was slim. Looking past the officers, soldiers ran in line while being yelled at. She went to grab Ethen by the hand and pull him away when it became their turn.

"Next!"

"We're here to join Queen Cillian's army. We overheard and it all sounds great. What do you think Kara?" Ethen faced her in excitement.

"Well, I…"

"I'm sorry, young lad," the officer interrupted, "you are too young and far too skinny. I'm not sure you could hold a blade properly, let alone attack. You'd be more of a liability. The queen does not desire young blood to be spilled. Maybe in a year or two. I hope that the rest of your generation is as brave as you are."

"But I practice with my sword all day. I only had a wooden one, but I swear I could defend myself. Please Sir," Ethen pleaded.

"I'm sorry son. We do not accept boys your age…" his gaze went to Kara. "Or ladies. I'm sorry. Try again next year."

The officer looked past Ethen to the next young man in line. Kara tried to pretend as bummed out. All she could muster was saying sorry.

"Give me a break. You're not sorry," Ethen scowled as he walked off.

"You're right, I'm not sorry because I didn't do anything. But what if this means we're not supposed to join some stupid army. I honestly don't remember ever having this much money before. Let's go get something to eat and we'll talk about it. Let's do something we both want to do. You smell that? I'm about to faint if I don't get something in me soon."

"Okay," Ethen said with a sigh.

Kara wanted to skip but kept her pace down to a jolly walk.

"What are you hungry for? Whatever you want little brother. Let's treat ourselves. This doesn't have to be as bad as you're making it. You heard the officer. It's like you don't care that you could get killed or me killed for that matter." Kara reached around Ethen's shoulder to bring him closer so she could tickle his side, forcing a smile.

"Stop it!" His smile flipped back to a frown.

"I saw a smile."

Ethen held firm.

"Never mind, you *can't* smile. You're not allowed to. That's right, *don't smile.*" Kara got in his face. "You better not smile, little brother. You smile and I swear you'll be sorry."

Ethen couldn't last any longer. He gave in with short laugh and a grin.

"I hate it when you do that," he said, pushing her away.

"Cheer up, will ya? For me? You truly can't think of any good reason *not* to join the military?"

"I guess you're right. I just want to make a difference in the world."

"I know what you mean." Her eyes drifted toward the town's circle. "Look, it's The Fishy School."

"Hey, you should see if they'll buy your songs," Ethen suggested.

"They're really good. Actually, *too* good. I'm sure they wouldn't be interested in my songs."

"Oh, come on. Your songs are good…"

"Ethen stop!" She grabbed Ethen. "That's Marx. He's the one that tied up all those guys."

Seeing Marx through the front window of a diner, Kara thought of the magical emblem that he supposedly carried. How much was it worth if all those men were hired to achieve it? As a scheme brewed, Ethen unknowingly assisted with an idea.

"I wonder if he could train us," he said.

"I bet he could." she decided to keep her intentions to herself. "You know, I'm sure Hallbert has a mind to steal that item that fat man talked about. What if we warned him? What if we asked him to train us for compensation?"

"You think that would work?" he asked.

"Doesn't hurt to try. Does this mean we know where we're eating because I'm about to eat my own hair if we don't pick soon."

"Sure, let's go."

They were greeted by a hostess who looked the siblings up and down with a suspicious eye. "Hi. Can I, umm, help you?"

"Table for two *ma'am*." Kara didn't hide her attitude.

"Sure, right this way."

Kara eyed Marx, engaged in a conversation with a young man. Empty plates and bowls implied they'd been there for a while. She was pleased to see several empty mugs as well. Anything that might impair Marx brought her closer to claiming that necklace for herself.

"You know Eddy?" the waitress asked, catching Kara's gaze. "They've been here all day talking. Let me know if you need anything," the hostess said as she turned to walk away; Kara grabbed her.

"We won't need any time. I'll have anything fried," Kara said.

"And I'll have that barbecued beef," Ethen said immediately after.

"Fried squid is one of our top dishes sold…" The hostess's awkward glance came with a pause. "I'm sorry but can I see payment? Some come in, eat and run."

Rolling her eyes, Kara showed more than enough to pay. "Fried squid sounds great. You got any dessert?"

"We have strawberry custard pie."

"We'll have two of those as well. Here, payment up front. Any chance we can get that pie first?" Kara handed her a steel coin. "Here, for your troubles."

"Thank you. I'll put that order in," the hostess accepted the coin and went back to the front.

"You going to talk to him?" Ethen asked.

"I'll make sure he doesn't leave. I feel like I need to eat first. The smell in here has me lightheaded."

Ethen nodded in agreement. The pies were served. The first two bites were eaten as fast as they were set down.

"I'm sure Hallbert has plans to try to get that necklace." Kara spoke between bites. "Marx probably has no idea that anyone would say anything about it. Or at least he doesn't think anyone would believe what they heard. Like Hallbert said, magical items are pretty rare. I don't know how many Hallbert knows who could get the word out. But if he's staying at The Gist tonight, that will give him time to plot and tell others. All he would need to do…"

"Look, it's Rifi and Kagu," Ethen interrupted. Kara scowled seeing that they, too, noticed Marx.

"Forget Hallbert, Rifi's just as capable, if not more so, stealing something on Marx's person." Kara stopped to think before she reached into her satchel and pulled out her parchment and pencil. "We can't let them see that we're here to warn Marx. Go distract them. Go say hi or something."

"I know those two. Well, not actually. I saw them miles east of here," Marx said.

"It's not every day you see a goblin and libby elf," Eddy slurred.

"Eddy, are you drunk?" Marx asked. "You should slow down. It's not even dusk."

"Ah, I'm alright. How many have you had?" Eddy asked.

"Two." Marx answered as Ethen greeted the elf and goblin. "Wait, I've seen him too."

"Can I help you, miss missy?" Eddy asked.

Marx turned to see Kara standing over him.

"Kara? Has the entire Hairy Barrel come to Laneloon?" Marx asked.

"Just read this." Kara laid a note on the table and walked out of the diner.

Marx read:

We met that bunch of mercenaries on the way here. There are others after your necklace. Meet me out back after I'm done eating and keep that thing safe.

Marx crumpled the paper as he cursed in silence. He didn't think anyone would believe what those men had to say, or that they would say anything themselves.

"What's that note say?" Eddy asked.

"Never mind."

"You filthy weasel," Eddy said with a wink and a laugh.

"You were saying something about your horse." Marx veered the conversation back to what it was.

"Oh yeah, my dear old Betsy. She died. Poor thing was running on her last leg after dad passed. Now I don't have a way to get my supplies from Fallwell. Just one more problem. Not sure how my father did it. Running a diner isn't as easy as you might think." Eddy went on about overhead calculations and how his lack of sleep will end up killing him like it did his dad.

Marx wasn't listening. His thoughts were dragged to what Kara knew. He had no choice but to wait until she was done eating. The thought arose: that it seemed this was the extended hand he thought of that morning.

Chapter Four
Set Sail to Bail

"Hey Rifi, what are you doing here?" Kara asked, stepping out of The Squirming Squid.

"Just walking my goblin. What are *you* guys doing here? I thought you were looking to get recruited," Rifi returned.

"We were turned down. I'm too young and too skinny." Ethen kicked the dirt.

"Ethone no meat. Bones see here." Kagu pointed to Ethen's midsection, agreeing he was far too skinny.

"Leaving the life isn't always as easy as it should be. I see you chose The Squirming Squid of all places to eat today." Rifi glanced at the window that showed Marx on the other side.

"Yeah, what of it?" Kara challenged.

Rifi lowered his voice and changed his mouth pattern from what he was really saying, a skill known by thieves to throw off those who have mastered lip reading. "Nothing other than we want in. I'm sure Hallbert is already putting together a team to be on the lookout for speedy there. Which means we have the advantage, for now. The only thing that oaf bests me at is knowing more people. So, rather than let him take the spoils, we should just spoil ourselves. What do you say?"

Kara looked to Ethen with a slightly raised eyebrow.

"Oh, all right. Look, I met him last night at the Barrel. We spoke before you even came in. Which means Ethen and I get sixty percent," Kara said.

"You don't have the ranking to propose mid-majority," Rifi replied.

"Not before now, I didn't. Look, we don't want him to get suspicious." Kara laughed and playfully shook Rifi's shoulder.

"Fine, what's the plan, *boss?*" Rifi asked.

"Just let me spend some time with him. I'll give the signal or send a note with more details of where he's staying." Kara raised her voice with a slap on Rifi's back. "You two take care. I'll see you back at the Barrel."

"Barrel bring grumbling dizzy face," Kagu said, grabbing his stomach.

Rifi said his farewell and pulled on Kagu's chains to move along.

Ethen and Kara came back to their table to find food waiting for them. Kara was happy that part of her plan involved filling her belly and giving her brain a break before it decided what to do.

"When was the last time we ate like this?" Kara sat and stuffed her mouth.

Ethen didn't answer until he swallowed.

"When mom was alive."

Kara's fork dropped.

"I didn't mean …" Ethen stumbled.

Their blemished past swept the room like an unwelcoming breeze and with it, images of their mother's last days, dying, sick and in bed. Kara was brought back to the middle of the night when her father woke her, snatched her up and rode off without letting her say goodbye. Earlier that day her parents had argued; voices rose high. The clash of harsh words ended with her mother's statement that silenced the room: *"I don't love you anymore."*

Years had passed when Kara caught word that not only had her mother remarried but she bore a boy, Ethen. She lit up at the thought and reality that she had a three-year-old baby brother. Although Kara's father forbade her from visiting her mother, she had every intention to know Ethen. When the opportunity was presented, she snuck out to meet him and even returned to visit him, and her mother, from time to time.

One visit, a familiar tension filled the home. Ethen's father had abandoned him and their mother to love another woman. Depressed, their mother lay in bed most days. Whether it was the lack of food or the will to live, no one was sure, but one day their mother fell ill, nonetheless. Six shorts months after and death claimed her; Ethen was only eight, Kara fifteen.

Ethen was taken into custody by an orphanage, one with terror stories told about it. Beatings, tiresome labor, and even starvation were common tales told, enough to inspire worry in little Kara. She pleaded with her father to take Ethen in. She repeated the stories, yet her father refused all the same. He said harshly yet plainly: *"I don't want the daily reminder of that woman lying with another man under my roof."* In that moment, Kara got the answer to the question she wondered all that time, *why did mom leave him?*

Much like her father who took her from her bed, she got the nerve in the middle of the night to run away, find Ethen, and care for him herself. Keeping to the shadows, she approached the orphanage, crept through a broken window and cupped Ethen's mouth when she woke him. She whispered an invitation to a new life. He nodded. The two fled west, to the villages outside Elmester. While some families helped her raise him early on, several turns of events later taught them how to steal to survive, eventually landing them at the Hairy Barrel.

Kara didn't mean to drop her fork. Part of her daily struggle was avoiding certain truths, so when reality came knocking, she sometimes froze, refusing to answer the door. She picked up the fork.

"It's okay," she said.

"I know you do your best and I know you told Rifi what he wanted to hear. Just like I know that part of you wants that necklace for yourself—so you can take care of us. But I don't think Vonnie knows what he was talking about. I think you really are sick of lying and stealing. We don't know that man over there, but I think he's an honest man—something that sticks out," Ethen said.

Kara thought of the first sign that Marx *was* an honest man and how she first felt about it. That he must be a naïve, unaware of the world's cruel intentions. But another thought, driven by curiosity, nudged her to think otherwise. Perhaps it was the world that was unaware of truths that she knew little about and that this man knew, things that ought to be.

"Vonnie *was* right about something. I'd be dim not to listen to ya." She smirked. "Once in a while anyways."

Kara made up her mind. A decision that not only brought back her appetite but lifted the heavy cloak she wore daily and flung it to the ground. She turned to Marx who happened to turn toward her. Their eyes locked.

"You're right little brother, no more lies."

The young man at Marx's table stood up as a waitress cleared their table. Marx's eyebrows rose, asking her if this was a good time to talk. She gulped down her glass of water, wiped her mouth, and nodded. The three met on the back patio.

"Hello Kara, and you're Ethen, right? Sorry, I overheard you talk yesterday at the tavern," Marx extended his hand.

"Yes Sir. And you're Marx," Ethen replied and shook.

Marx faced Kara. "What is it you know?"

"That you have some magical necklace, that it gives you super speed. At least that's what Hallbert guessed. Which, by the way, is why you're in trouble. He knows this city pretty good and enough people in it to get what he wants. Unless you feel like tying up a hundred thieves, I'd say you're knee deep in a river full of hassle."

"Why are you helping me?"

"Because we want you to train us," Ethen spoke quickly, over whatever his sister might try to concoct.

"That's right," Kara said. "We want out of this town and out of this life. Look, we steal to live, and we want to change all that. We can help you escape and tell you what to look out for. Maybe you train my little brother and get me somewhere I can make coin with my songs. It was *your* advice to start somewhere other than the Barrel and Laneloon is no longer an option. So, what do you say?"

Before Marx could reply, Kara continued.

"Either way, we are happy to help. I'm doing this to clear my conscience, you might say."

She glanced at her brother and was happy to see him smile.

"I first want to thank you for your honesty, *if* you are being honest. *And* if you are, I will greatly consider your proposal," Marx said.

"Really? Just like that?" Kara asked.

"The greatest historical events begin with moments *just like that*. I told you before, I tend to go where the wind takes me. And I think I feel a breeze, but not quite enough to take me to the skies. Not yet. Now, if you'll excuse me, I need to speak with my horse. Meet me in the circle across the street in a few hours."

"Okay. Hey, be careful. Remember what I told you. These guys are everywhere and have more ways to get what they want outside the average pickpocket. Understand?" she said.

"I'll be careful. Thanks." Marx walked inside.

As he made his way back in, he saw Eddy.

"I'm beat, I came in early and those few drinks slowed me," Eddy said.

"Go on then, get some rest. I'm happy to have caught up and I'm sorry about your father. He was a good man, well *mostly*." The laugh reminded them of Pete.

"Thanks. I live on the second story. You'll see it? Attached to the back end of the diner?" Eddy pointed. "Come visit anytime."

"Will do."

Walking outside, Marx heard the last strum of the last song of the Fishy School as the crowd applauded. He greeted his horse.

"Hey boy, sorry about that. Saw an old friend. Actually, in a way, I met a new friend. Unfortunately, the friend I hoped for had passed on to the next life."

Ages snorted, giving his condolences.

"I appreciate it. Pete will be missed, but his son is a spitting image of his old man. I guess one could say he's Pete's gift to the world."

A yellow blur caught the side of his eye, dulling the other colors of the day. There she was again. The same woman he saved and the same woman that visited him in his dream that morning. She went along with the crowd as it dispersed. Her dark red hair flared in the sun, brightening with a metallic shimmer. He stared, not noticing her walking toward him. He was caught as their eyes met. He turned and instantly turned back to see if she had noticed. A flashed grin affirmed she did.

"Are you following me?" she asked.

"I suppose, in a way, I am. But not in the way you'd think. Those guys are pretty good." Marx nodded toward the stage.

"Ah, they *are* fun. Sorry I was off-putting last night. I should have given my name. It's Elet. Um, Mark, is it?"

"Marx."

"That's right. Thank you again for saving me." As her long eyelashes lowered, her brown irises beneath were targeted on him.

"Think nothing of it. I hope you're okay from such an event."

"I'll be fine. If anything, it left me to be better prepared next time. Believe me, the lesson was learned."

The two stood staring. The long silence was noticed; Elet's smile softened the awkward pause.

"So, did you ever find the man you were looking for?" Marx asked.

"You might say that. Although it was uneventful, my time wasn't wasted, as I'm sure it never is."

"I have a similar view on life. But that leaves me with a question, do you believe in destiny?"

She pondered a moment. "I'm not sure anyone can truly define *destiny*. If it's defined as what's outside our control, it's safe to assume we have no true understanding of what it actually means."

Marx chuckled. "Fair enough. With that said, do you believe in things you don't fully understand?"

"Like what?" Her eyelashes dropped and rose twice.

Marx searched for an answer other than the obvious—*love*.

"I'm sorry, Marx, but I am leaving this place this evening, so I know this is sudden, but I must ask, are you held here at Laneloon?"

"Why do you ask?"

"I need an escort up the northern strait. A man of your skills could come in handy. That is, if you're capable of doing what you did last night. Would you be that escort?

"I'm sorry. I shouldn't have assumed you are some muscle-for-hire. After last night and the crew I decided to sail with .… It's just that I now have reason to be more cautious and something tells me I can trust you. Figured there's no harm in asking. I can pay more than enough for your time and travel."

"Where are you needing to go?" he asked.

"Stumpford."

"You're kidding."

"No. Why do you say that?"

"I have some old friends up there. What about you? Are you friends with halflings?"

"Not exactly. We'd travel three days inland from there. Near Lemwven."

"Lemwven, huh? What business do you have there?"

"I'm afraid it's private. Not that it will put you in any more danger, I assure you. Quite the contrary."

"I see." Marx thought for a moment. "I may be willing *if* I can bring two with me. They shouldn't be any trouble. One is a girl, nineteen, and another is her younger brother, about twelve. No more than a moment before I came out to talk to Ages here, I was offered a similar request. Will that be a problem?"

"I don't mind. However, the crew I'm sailing with aren't the most prestigious bunch. But they're the only ones traveling in the direction I need to go as the sun sets."

"That's fantastic. The prestigious can be boring."

"Is that a yes, then?"

"It's a strong gust of wind, that for sure."

"Beg your pardon?"

"Nothing. It's almost a yes." Marx gave Ages a sad rub-of-the-nose before turning toward the Squirming Squid. "If you don't mind, I'll be right back."

"Do what you must. I'll be at the southern docks." She looked down at her dress. "I'll be hard to miss. No later than dusk now."

"Yes ma'am."

Marx arrived at Eddy's front door and gave it a knock, Eddy answered.

"Eddy, I wanted to give you a gift. You said you were down a horse. Well, as fate would have it, I need to part with my loyal companion, Ages. Will you promise me you will take good care of him?" Marx asked.

"Really? You sure?"

"Only if you promise."

"Sure, I promise."

"He enjoys conversations and is a good listener."

Eddy's smile assumed he was jesting; Marx's stare assured he wasn't.

"Sure, no problem. I need someone to talk to on the long road to Fallwell."

"Good, here. Follow me." Marx led Eddy to the center of town and introduced him to his horse. He squeezed in a couple of stories that reflected not only daring adventures but of a deep-seated relationship between man and steed. Eddy felt compelled and even duty bound to live up to his promises.

* * * * *

"You think Marx is really going to train me?" Ethen asked his sister as they walked the shops.

"I don't know. He seemed pretty serious." Kara grinned as one shop came into view. Turning toward Ethen, her eyebrows jumped up and down.

"What is it?" he asked.

"You need a sword to train with. And we have enough to get you one. It won't be anything fancy but a shy better than the wooden one you had."

"Are you serious?"

"To make up for all the cold meals." She pushed Ethen playfully.

"Stop it. You've done fine. And I'll never forget what you gave up to do so," he replied, shoving her back before starting a race with a sprint.

Kara ran after him. Turning into the shop, they both ran right into a wall named Hallbert. He towered over the two as if expecting them. The straight face he wore came with an uneasy smile.

"Hey Hallbert," Kara said.

"You guys getting recruited?" he asked.

"Ethen is too young for recruitment."

"That's too bad. Now that you ain't joining an army, you interested in some work? I asked around and that *item,* those buffoons were after, is worth a high bit more than what I originally assumed. Enough to let you guys in on the profit. Even enough to get you two a cottage in the woods if you play your cards right. Interested?" Hallbert's dead stare was unmoved. "We know you spoke with him out back of the Squid. Rifi just told me. He figured he'd tell me to gain some information. He is tracking him as we speak. You will not be getting mid-majority, but I assure you, I can negotiate a far better price than you could ever. Which means you'll be getting more than you thought and not nearly as much work. What do you say?"

Before Ethen gave away his answer, Kara spoke.

"Ethen, that's everything we've ever wanted. Plus, we are in over our heads." Kara's eyebrow rose slightly.

"Our own cottage? No foolin?" Ethen played along.

"Boy, with the amount I was told that thing is worth, you can one for each of you. Here, to sweeten the deal, I get you this sword." Hallbert placed his hand on a short sword hung on the wall. "I know you guys gained his trust. Something those men in the woods never had."

Ethen looked at Kara, who shrugged her shoulders as if to suggest, *go for it.*

"*And* this shield?" Ethen pointed.

"You little swindler, ha. You drive a hard bargain. Fine, the shield as well, but *only* if you get him to sleep in The Gist tonight. Deal?"

"That shouldn't be too hard. He said he was looking for an inn to rest in tonight. I could sway his decision," Kara said, pointing at a rare knife encased in glass, decorated with ruby roses. "Throw in this knife and you got yourself a deal."

* * * * *

The sun drifted across the sky in its last hour of the day. Shadows inherited most of the harbor, hinting at night's unavoidable darkness. On the dock's side of the city, the sun was still shining on those under it. Sailors tied up their ships at the docks while others carried their boats from the shore. At the southern docks, one small ship, titled the Path of Righteousness, was getting ready to set sail. The only two sailors were making preparations while their captain searched the streets. His eyes rested at ease when he found a beautiful woman in a yellow dress approach him.

"So, you've decided to join us today?"

"Yes. Thank you for waiting, Captain Larker. If you don't mind waiting a little while longer, I have company coming as well." Elet handed him a small stack of coin. "For any extra trouble."

Seeing gold, he smiled, baring his teeth coated with their own gold, as if welcoming home a missed relative. His blue eyes shone brightly in contrast to his ebony skin; a rare feature that mirrored his character. A combination of matted and braided hair was tied together, hung over one side of his shoulders, and fell past his knees. Each braid was decorated with beads, each telling a story of ventures across the seas. A worn leather vest, ripped and torn, was held together by sewn-in patches. Underneath, his shirt was on the verge of unthreading. Where his clothes failed to convince anyone of his expertise, he made up for it with confidence in language and posture.

"Please, missy, call me Skye," he urged. The bright sky behind his matching eyes was a reminder of his name.

"Excuse me. Skye. Well, I'm all gathered up. My guest should arrive before dusk. Would you mind? Those are my belongings there." Elet gestured to her bag laid next to the small ship.

"My pleasure." Skye said softly before he shouted, startling Elet. "Kork! Come get the lady here's bag."

A gnome arrived at the average height of two and a half feet. Muscular, as far as gnomes go, he scanned for the bag as though he was ready to wrestle it. Large eyes, nose and mouth; gnome's facial expressions appear exaggerated compared to the other races. Gray hair gave away his later years of around two hundred, but his pep was spry. His eyebrows furrowed, his bottom lip balled at the captain's shouts.

Noticing his height, Elet interjected. "Oh, allow me."

"Missy, I wouldn't…" Skye tried to warn her.

"I got it!" Kork said defensively.

"I'm terribly sorry. I didn't mean…"

The gnome's stare told her to save it.

Skye laughed as he raised his hand toward the ship. "After you, Missy."

* * * * *

At the town's circle, Kara and Ethen met with Marx. Marx gave Ages a last farewell and a hug. Ages snorted his farewell and stomped the ground as if to wave goodbye.

"So? Did you make a decision?" Kara asked.

"Yes. I have decided to train Ethen and travel with you two up north to Stumpford. I have friends near there so that's a place to get your song noticed. Tungsten's Echo and Lemwven are just a couple of large cities within a few days' travel from there. That means more ears to hear what you have to offer. And I think the halflings and hill dwarves there will like your style. They're fans of human culture and that song I heard captures human humor well. I believe this is your way out. What do you say?"

Kara looked to her brother, who bobbed his head in acceptance.

"I can't believe I'm going to say it. Sure, let's do it." She tried not to get too excited. She searched for any spy's eyes she was sure was on them. She leaned in to whisper. "There are more people involved than I thought. The sooner we get out of here, the better."

"I've really made a mess of things. I should have fled those numbskulls. My rambunctious behavior never served me well. The item I carry is most precious. It cannot fall into the wrong hands. You must not say anything to anyone any further. The necklace and its secret must remain safe. The thieves in town don't have the slightest idea what they are agreeing to."

"As long as it pays well, they'd sell their own mother's medicine," Kara said.

They arrived at the southern docks. It wasn't hard for Marx to spot Elet's dress. Her back turned to him, she stood on a small ship, facing the setting sun. As he approached the gangway, a dark-skinned man with striking blue eyes greeted him.

"You missy's company? We'd been waiting for ya. Ah, little whippers." Skye eyed the siblings. "All welcome. Come now. Haste is key."

"Much appreciated," Marx said as he bowed slightly. "I'm Marx, this is Kara and Ethen."

"Captain Skye Larker, at your service." Skye returned with a heavy bow.

Elet must not have heard the introduction as she remained facing the sun.

"Elet, we made it. I have some friends I'd like you to meet," Marx said.

A green and red bird flew from Elet's hands as she turned and smiled.

"Were you just holding that bird?" Kara asked, amused.

"The birds and I understand each other. They have advised the waters and skies are clear up ahead, which means we get to enjoy the stars tonight." Elet came, offering her hands that cupped Kara's. "I sure am glad I now have a lady friend. No offense, Sir Marx."

"None taken. I understand completely," Marx replied, glancing at the contrast of brute and beauty on board.

"Nice to meet you. I'm Kara." She looked around. "We've never been on a boat before."

"And who is this strapping young man? A sword *and a* shield? I didn't know I was paying for *two* bodyguards." Elet gripped Ethen's shoulder. "Worth every expense, I'm sure."

"This is Ethen. I have vowed to train him on our way up north. I hope you don't mind," Marx said.

"Not at all."

Chained links made a racket as the anchor rose. Kara's heart thumped at the reality of leaving behind her life of lies, struggles to eat, and stealing to do so. She was afraid to look back in case Hallbert was there staring, which made her look all the more. Instead, she saw Rifi and Kagu taking full notice.

No one, however, took notice of a boy in bright orange trousers running up to a guard and offering him a piece of paper. On it, a drawing of a dark-skinned man with blue eyes. *Piracy* stood out to the guard along with a reward of five hundred gold coin—*alive.* The boy pointed to a man on the docks who fit the description, observing his boat from several angles as if readying his departure. The guard signaled his comrades who quickly surrounded him. Skye turned, noticing the guards and his chances of escaping growing narrow by the second.

"Hoist those sails! Or we spend the night in a cell or the gallows," Skye yelled over the guard's whistles and shouting.

"Sail. We only have one," Kork corrected.

Skye lifted the gangway. A set of guards had already brought their own; longer, with hooks at the end to stop the small ship from moving. They hooked successfully. The guards made their way on board as Kork snickered. He grabbed what looked like a bomb and rubbed its wick. It fizzled before he rolled it under the uninvited guards about to board.

"I'd stay back if I were you," Kork advised Elet and her company.

The bomb did not explode but wheezed. Thick smoke rose from under the guards, giving them no choice but to inhale it. They felt a sudden shift in reality. Something slithered under their skin. Then came the warped perception of gravity and finally the hallucinations.

"This is my favorite part." Kork tried holding back his laughter.

Fireworks shot out as the men screamed in horror as they jumped into the water beneath them.

"The gangway!" Skye yelled as he tried to detach it while avoiding the smoke.

"We're hooked. What have I taught you about leverage?" Kork said, annoyed.

Using two knives, one of his and one snatched from Skye's boot, Kork placed the blades under the hooks and pulled back. The hooks separated themselves just enough for him to fling them off, causing the gangway, and any guards still on it, to fall into the water below. He lifted himself up to catch a glimpse of the guards splashing around in distress. His laughter forced him to drop back down. Skye snickered before turning to face another mate of his, the only one not yet introduced.

"Phin, do you mind?" Skye asked.

In an attire similar to Skye's, a man in his late fifties started chanting while stretching his left, ring covered hand forward and his right, cupped hand, against his shoulder. Continuing muttering strange words, he lifted his left index and middle finger and pushed his right hand forward. His long, straggly black and gray hair, and matching beard, blew back as the ship surged forward.

Kara looked back to see Rifi and Kagu shoot her a confused look. She smirked, shrugged her shoulders, and twirled her gaze ahead, allowing the wind to blow directly on her face as the ship sailed into the open sea.

"Yes, a *strong* gust of wind," she heard Marx mutter to himself.

Chapter Five
Captain Skye Larker's Fate & Mates

"Where are you taking us? You are supposed to take us up north, not south!" Elet shouted.

"My apologies, missy. We'll need to make a slight detour first. Don't worry, I'll make good on our agreement," Skye replied as he looked back at the harbor.

"Why are they after you? What did you do?" Elet pressed.

"Honestly? I'm not sure. I wasn't always the same gentleman you see now. Forty percent will be knocked off for the delay." Skye peered through his spyglass toward pursuit behind them.

Elet stepped close to Marx and whispered, "You may have to do something. We'll end up getting hanged along with them."

Marx nodded in understanding; his hand crept toward his hilt.

"Not so fast." Kork uncorked a bottle and pulled his arm back. "This is that same chemical that turned those fearless guards into screaming children. Actually, it's an extract, about ten times stronger. All is well. Just listen to the captain. We're just making a quick stop for the next few nights, so please drop your blades and kick them over. All of you."

Kara shot Marx a look, *the necklace*. He shook his head and did as he was told. The rest followed.

"You'll be alright. If we *do* get caught, I'll make sure to let the govies know you're innocent. We may even tie you up for appearances," Skye assured.

"*Is* it only appearances?" Marx asked.

"Here they come!" Skye yelled before answering. "I understand your position; I do. All that I ask is you understand mine. They mean to hang me and my crew. Now whether we deserve such extreme punishment is up for debate. We will either be stripped of our right to speak or our argument will be dismissed, regardless of what we say. Either way, we're dead men.

"You understand? It's not right, yet they call it justice. Although you may yield to the govies, I only yield to the sea and to the gods."

"Crew?" Marx looked at the two other men. "How long can your friend aid this ship's speed? It's our only chance to outsail them. I probably don't need to tell you, but magic alone is worth the noose, or worse."

He eyed Marx, then smiled. "We have the sea and our wit. They haven't failed me yet. Does this mean we can trust each other?"

"Where are we going?"

"Rimcaster. There, I'll find you and your company a way to Stumpford—per my agreement with the lady. And if we're looking like we won't make it, we'll tie you all up for appearances."

"You can trust me," Marx assured.

"You don't mind that we keep your steel, do you? Keep my mates' minds at ease."

"As long as we don't need them, I don't see why not." Marx stood next to Elet.

"What's going on?" she asked.

"Looks like we are going to Rimcaster," Marx said. "They *will* hang these men and might even turn in that wizard to the Five High Council where I hear they do much worse. Whichever way we look at it, we're not in a position to barter. Best we stay on their good side. If the harbor's men catch us, we'll play hostage. Which is true, more or less."

"And you think they'll listen?"

"They *did* take our weapons, and I have no arrest record, do you?"

"No."

"Then all we can do is hope. I believe our survival is best on this course."

Elet looked back toward the Harbor then returned to Marx. "I trust you."

An hour and a half passed since the veil of night crossed the sky. Phin, exhausted, rested as the ship slowed down significantly.

"Good job, Phin. How far did that spell take us?" Skye asked.

"About fifty miles," Phin answered between heavy breaths.

"Will that give us the edge we need?"

Phin smiled and Skye nodded.

A couple more hours passed. The night was lit by Lux, one of two Iris moons. Lux set the ocean on fire with her violet glow, dwarfing her ember of a brother, Dante. She drifted across the northern sky, hovering over the harbor's ship that pursued Skye and his crew. At first, the sails were nothing more than a speck but grew larger by each passing moment.

Elet's bird friend was correct; the sky was clear. The dimmer stars were lost while Lux flaunted her bright glow. Still, the brightest stars seen were enough where Skye didn't need his compass. He stared at the Laneloon vessel that grew, ten times in size. He met with Kork and Phin in private before approaching Marx and Elet.

"I have spoken with my mates. We do not intend to put you or your company in any more danger than we already have. I am sorry for the inconvenience that we have caused already." He looked at Marx. "We will not make it to Rimcaster fast enough and so maybe it will be best that *you* tie *me* up," Captain Skye Larker said. "You will need to convince them you overthrew us and lit this here lantern to alert them." Skye lit the lantern nearby and turned its knob to its brightest potential. "We're tired of running. Maybe we need to face our past."

"If we do this, we cannot convince them of a fair trial," Marx said.

Marx looked at the wizard, who appeared to be a nice enough fellow. He had heard some of the gruesome stories of those who were caught practicing the ancient magical arts. So harsh were the stories, the punishments never seemed justified.

"I have spoken to my mates, and we all agree we must face what we've been running from. Our fate, as it always is, is in the sea's hands. Those ships have cannons. Not sure if you'd seen those in action, but they will tear apart an entire city, let alone this small vessel. Our decision is final, so promise me not to intervene." Skye's tone was firm.

"Fine," Marx agreed grimly.

Skye turned to Elet. "I'm truly sorry missy; we weren't able to get you where you needed to go." Skye's failure was hard to hide.

"I'll figure something out when we get back." Elet's face softened at the bravery.

"I'm going to spend the rest of my free time with my men. Don't forget your weapons. Give me just a few moments before you tie us up?" Skye walked away.

"Are they really going to be hanged?" Kara asked.

"Unfortunately, for the trouble they put those Laneloon guards in, I'm sure of it," Marx replied.

"We have to save them," Ethen urged.

"I'm not so sure we can," Marx said.

The four sat in silence, trying to think this situation through. Kara, Ethen, and Marx knew trouble back at Laneloon wasn't just for Skye and his mates, but for them as well. Marx knew his necklace couldn't fall into the wrong hands. He excused himself to the stern, got on his knees, and prayed. With Skye's request and the death that faced them, he didn't feel right about letting them hang. When he prayed, his convictions were confirmed.

The ship trailing behind was well within view. Marx approached Skye and his mates huddled close to each other.

"It's time to tie us up. Hurry now." Skye kicked a pile of rope at his side.

"Okay, but I want to help you escape once we get back. I too yield to the gods. I feel they want me to help you," Marx said.

"I'd be lying to say that I wasn't touched, truly. But I asked you not to intervene and I, *we*, mean it. And you agreed." Skye remained firm.

"Just let us help," Marx pressed. Skye grinned yet shook his head.

Kork and Phin shook their heads as well. Joining them, Marx shook his head, but due of their stubbornness. Reluctantly, he agreed before tying them up.

"May the gods show you mercy." Marx turned and shouted, "Hey, help us!" He waved his hands toward the approaching ship. He spoke low to Elet and the siblings. "Raise your hands. They might shoot you. Let me do the talking."

He yelled across. "Don't shoot. We took over the ship and tied up the ones who escaped. We lit this lantern to show you where we are."

A soldier returned. "Keep your hands raised and come as close as you can. No sudden movements. Where are the others?"

"They are tied up in the back of the ship," Marx advised.

"Stay right where you are. Rest your hands over the taffrail. We're coming aboard."

Crossbows pointed while a gangway hooked the ship. Soldiers boarded, swords in hand.

A man, set apart in uniform, walked up to Marx. "They're in the back, you say?"

"Yes, back there," Marx pointed as the uniform never took his eyes off him.

"They're here, Sir. And they're tied up," a soldier yelled.

"Impressive. We will have questions for you on board." He turned to the rest. "Each of you. If you don't mind, that way."

Boarding the larger ship, they were met with aimed crossbows. The captain, singled out by his own unique uniform and multiple pendants, waited until they were brought to him.

"Please hand over your weapons if you don't mind," the captain requested. They each handed over their weapons that they had just gotten back. The captain continued. "How was it you overthrew these men?"

"I had a chance to seize them, and I took it. I am efficient in combat, Sir," Marx answered.

"Then we better shackle you up. You will have your hearing back at the harbor. Pip, put them all in the brig," the captain commanded.

"Aye, Captain," Pip replied.

The captain waved them away before Marx could protest. Shackles came next before descended into the hull.

Next, Skye, Kork and Phin were pulled in front of the captain.

"Captain Skye Larker, is it? With features such as yours, I'm surprised you've gotten away this long. You will pay capital punishment for what you've done." The captain wasn't hiding his enjoyment.

"And what is it I did?" Skye asked.

The captain laughed. "Does it matter, scum? Your warrant says piracy for five hundred gold. Not bad. But I say you will each hang dead for what you did to our men back at the harbor. Whatever lawless spree you've been on, it has met its end. Now, who was it that cast that spell?"

Each was silent.

"Mutes, huh? You all know the darkness that the wizards had brought into this world and yet you wish to protect it. No matter. We have ways of knowing and judgement *will* be carried out to those who dabble in such wickedness. Shackle them each and bind all their mouths. No more spells tonight. And do not spare any pain you might inflict before we get back. We aren't allowed such pleasure at the harbor." The captain flicked his wrist and turned away.

Ahead, downstairs, Marx and his company were shoved to meet Pip's pace as they passed the crew. Any eyes that could stare did. One ragged crew member turned a corner, nearly running into the prisoners.

"Out of the way Jerry!" Pip yelled at the humble man, nearly kicking him. He quickly scurried out of the way with a salute.

"Sorry, Sir. My apologies, Sir," Jerry replied, eyes averted.

The other soldiers added their own remarks, *"Move swab"* and *"Ye seagull shite."*

On the lowest deck was the brig—metal grated walls with locks on their doors. An area that shared buckets of urine and feces. Seemingly, the buckets had not yet been thrown overboard from the ship's last voyage. Breaths were held over the stench. Marx tried to protest, asking Pip if this was necessary. Pip replied with one last shove into Marx's new cell. Skye came next, shoved inside the cell next to him.

Once everyone was imprisoned, Pip turned. Walking up to the pair of guards stationed the bottom of the stairs, he barked, ensuring that they kept the prisoners caged.

"Aye, aye Sir," they replied.

"Tight ship," Marx said.

Gagged, Skye shrugged as if to say, *what did you expect?*

"Yuck! It smells worse than the Barrel," Kara said.

"Why do they have buckets of poo?" Ethen said, plugging his nose.

"Part of the treatment I'm sure," Elet said as she turned to Marx. "You sure we'll be treated fairly back at Laneloon?"

"I believe so," Marx replied, although that idea was dwindling.

"I wonder if Hallbert will be sore that we took off," Ethen said.

As much as Kara wanted to avoid the worst, her thoughts tugged her back into worry. It wasn't Hallbert or the thieves she feared, but the idea that freedom was a luxury she could never afford. The rush of the open sea would soon become a reminder of what wasn't hers. It seemed she couldn't escape her past life, apparently even if she sailed away from it. That no matter the outcome, her destiny was already written. One that involved stealing to scrape by and a poor caretaker for her brother.

As the worried thoughts whispered, the cell walls closed in, mirroring her suffocated soul, desperate to escape. She found a strange comfort staring into the black-inked shadows pooling across the brig. Lost in defeat, she nearly missed two pairs of pointed ears and beady eyes hidden within the darkness. Two faces crept into view.

"Rifi? Kagu?" She cupped her mouth as she spoke.

Looking to see if the guards noticed, she breathed relief before turning to Ethen. Nudging her head, she signaled to look. The dark shadows hid the lily elf and goblin well, but after staring long enough, Ethen saw them too. A pair of small hands signaled back; something to do with taking care of the guards before anything else.

"What are you doing?" Marx whispered.

Kara put her finger to her mouth to keep him quiet. Marx followed their attention into the shadows but saw nothing. A moment passed before he saw a foot, the size of a child, or a lily elf. The foot darted back out of sight.

"Kara, no," Marx whispered. "If they help us escape, we'll *then* be in real trouble that we can't walk away from. I know our position seems dim, but you have to trust me."

A voice came from the top of the stairway, so Marx hushed up. It was the one they called Jerry. Seeing how he was treated up above, he halfway expected the guards to belittle him as well. They remained quiet. He walked up to the cell that held Skye who stood up and leaned against the door. Pulling free a knife, Jerry cut loose the binding around his mouth. The guards remained unmoved.

"Where are we?" Skye asked.

"We should be close enough. However, I haven't heard or seen anything yet," Jerry replied.

"Then why are you down here?"

"For orders. What do we do if we don't engage?"

"Oh Joni, ye have so little faith. We'll engage. Now that you *are* down here. Is everything in place?" Skye asked.

"Yes Sir."

"Then we can't risk getting found out yet. Go back up and double your rounds. Suspicion is our only weakness. And Joni, you've done good so far and assuming everything goes as planned, you'll be ranked boatswain. You've deserved it." Skye lowered his head in respect.

"Aye. Thank you, Sir. You'll receive the signal soon enough," Joni said before he hustled past the unmoved guards and up the stairs.

"Oui, Sammy," Skye whispered loudly in the guard's direction.

One of them turned. "Yes Sir?"

"How's your moms? Did she receive the medicine and payment?"

"Yes Sir. Thank ye Sir. She is better than ever," Sammy said.

"Good to hear lad. I hear she is as sweet as a boiled sugar plum. Stay in character a wee bit more, and you'll be able to see her indefinitely."

"Aye Sir," Sammy replied, joy found in him.

Skye turned to see four transfixed faces staring in his direction.

"What? You think I'd let myself get caught by these foul govies. Prepare to witness a ploy, a year in the making." Skye came close as he could to Marx's cell and stared into his eyes. "You were tested back there, and I'm glad I don't have to strip you and leave you stranded. Who knows? We might be looking to offer you a job."

He turned to Elet. "And you missy. I told you I'd get you up the northern strait and I intend to. I'm sorry for the delay, but what you were paying, I couldn't say no. Are we good?"

"I'm not so sure," Elet said, still stupefied.

The guards' faces turned to stone as they started approaching.

"At ease gents. Let me handle this," Skye moved closer to Elet. "I will offer you half off for the inconvenience. It just so happens we have trades up there as well. We both know you wouldn't be able to leave until tomorrow anyways, *if* you were lucky enough and definitely not for that price."

"*If* I'm not hanged in the process," Elet scowled.

"A fair point. Let's continue this conversation after I'm made captain of this fine vessel."

"Fine," she huffed.

After Kara and Ethen looked at each other and then back into the shadows. The beady eyes and small feet were gone.

Joni patrolled each floor with a bucket of filthy water and a scrub brush as he normally did. He locked eyes with certain men on each level as he made his way up to the main deck. Studying the stars, he noted they were headed back as fast as the wind would allow. Seeing no eyes on him, he snuck to the stern in hopes to see what he'd been waiting for. He knew that soon enough they'd be too far, and this entire operation would be for nothing. Stepping out of the light, his eyes adjusted to the darkness and stared out into the sea. The ends of his mouth rose.

"Swab! What are you doing back there? I seriously doubt you have scrubbed the entire lower deck. Get back down there," Pip yelled.

"Extremely sorry, Sir. Felt a bit queasy. I thought a bit of fresh air might help is all," Joni replied.

"*You* thought? I'm not so sure that pea brain ever mustered up a thought in your entire life. Back downstairs," Pip demanded.

"Aye, Sir. A hundred more apologies," Joni said as he hurried down the stairs.

Ignoring his orders, he darted to a particular area on the second deck. The heel of his boot fell hard; he stomped four times in a unique rhythm. Two men below departed from their station to send a signal of their own to the deck below them.

Skye, Kork and Phin looked at each other, grinning as they stood up. Sammy pulled out a ring of keys as he made his way over. Shouts were heard; whistles were blown. Feet pounded on every level as men hustled to their stations. Next came the sudden shift of the ship turning once again. Soon, everyone on board either saw or heard—pirates were approaching.

"Powder and shot!" Pip yelled to his officers, readying the ship's forty cannons. He stood next to his captain.

"Those fools must not know what we're capable of. Rarely has anyone witnessed cannons in action before, let alone attack a ship armed with them," the captain said amused. "We'll tear them in half on the first go. Just as we practiced, Pip."

"Aye, Sir." Pip replied.

The cannons' necks were filled with powder and cannonballs tightly pushed down.

"Ready to fire, Sir," a soldier shouted.

"Hold," Pip said. "Raise the gunports!" he yelled.

Each hatch was raised; cannons protruded from the ship.

"Light the linstocks!"

The approaching ship was close enough to see faces, raised blades, and notched arrows.

"Aim! Fire!" Pip yelled.

A long pause ended with nothing.

"Fire!" he yelled again, this time a squeal escaped him.

Still nothing.

"What in the depths is happening?!" he screamed.

"They aren't firing, Sir," a soldier reported.

"I've put that together, you sorry sack! Why aren't they firing?"

"I don't know, Sir," the soldier replied.

"Everyone, ready to fight. Draw your swords and aim your crossbows," the captain yelled as he drew his blade, making his way down the stairs. "I'll be in my cabin."

Once he reached the lower deck, he saw several daunting eyes track him.

"What are you looking at?" he yelled. "Back to your stations!"

A closer look and he saw blades drawn on other soldiers. A pair of men raised their crossbows toward the captain.

"Back up to the main deck, Sir," one of his soldiers told him.

The captain didn't wait; he ran back upstairs.

"We are being turned on. Quick fire on the men behind me!" The captain yelled.

Some soldiers tried shooting their crossbows with no such luck, while others pointed theirs at the ones struggling.

"Our crossbows won't fire!" one shouted.

When soldiers went for their swords, they found blades at their throats. "*Traitors!*" they scoffed. Pirates swung on ropes over, landing in front of their unarmed enemies. The takeover was sudden and barely expected. So much so that the pirates that boarded had little to do.

One pirate came up to the captain. "Something the matter with your guns?"

The captain, Pip, and the few who knew little of what was going on were corralled and herded like helpless sheep.

"There's nothing wrong with the guns. But if I were you, *Captain*, I'd look to get a return on that black powder. It's a bit feeble." Captain Skye Larker emerged from underneath, with Kork and Phin behind him. "And I must say, you should treat your crew with more respect."

The newly arrived pirates gathered around Skye as he raised his hands. The sleeves of a long black coat were placed over his elevated arms as the rest of the heavy leather wrapped around him. A lit pipe was set in one hand while a wine-filled chalice in the other. Finally, an intricately stitched leather hat with a long red feather was placed on top of his head. He took a few long gulps that emptied his cup, and then he puffed his pipe. The glow ignited his blue eyes that stared at the captain as his gold teeth shined when he smiled, smoke bellowing out.

"Show off," Kork said, rolling his large eyes.

Chapter Six

Captive Swap

"Bring a spring about!" Skye shouted as the ship, once again, turned around back south.

Pirates who invaded Laneloon's ship returned to theirs while others stayed aboard the newly acquired vessel. Skye eyed his prisoners. Taking his time, he studied each one. In the dark, his gold teeth shined, and his blue eyes glowed with help of the few lanterns. The effect came: that he could stare into the poor souls who dared stare back. His eyes ended on the previous captain.

"What's your name?" Skye asked.

"Captain Katzgood," he replied, standing tall.

"But you're not the captain anymore, are ya?"

"What do you plan to do with us?" Katzgoode asked.

"I *have* decided. And that is, it's not going to be up to me. Joni!" Skye yelled.

Joni, known to Katzgoode and his men as Jerry, walked up the stairs. His skittish steps were now confident. His nervous, apologetic face was now calm and cool. It was as if another spirit possessed the one they once called *swab*.

"Jerry?" Katzgoode asked.

"You must not have heard the Captain, *Captain*. My name is Joni, and you have me to thank for this mutiny," Joni ended his walk to stare at Katzgoode face-to-face.

Katzgoode's face flushed a few layers red. Not a breath escaped; instead, it built up like a fuming volcano. Joni laughed while Skye and the rest joined in.

Joni lifted his hand, palm open, as a sword was placed in it by another pirate. Katzgoode's anger suddenly lost itself as death knocked on his soon-to-be future.

"You're still nothing but a swab to me, boy," Katzgoode spoke between clenched teeth.

The blade was raised to Katzgoode's throat. He closed his eyes. After a moment of nothing, he opened them to see not the sword's end pointed at him but its handle.

"Take it," Joni said.

Confused, he looked around to see what kind of game was being played.

"Captain Skye Larker, I wish for you to let these men go at Rimcaster if the old captain cuts me down, as all of you are witness to," Joni dropped the sword at Katzgoode's feet, pulling free his own. "I want his death to be earned, not given."

The pirates cheered, and Skye grinned, satisfied.

"Aye, lad, you have my word," Skye said before he yelling, "Everyone make room!"

A circle formed, followed by chants and some bets. Not fully convinced of the gesture, Katzgoode picked up the sword at his feet. Gripping the hilt and studying the blade's weight added confidence. Although it had been many years since he used a blade seriously, he held firm the idea that he would kill this traitor. As he held the blade upward and centered, years of training came back to him, training that began and ended before Joni was old enough to properly pick up a blade. He didn't waste time putting it to use.

He lunged forward. His upper strike was parried, just as planned. He shifted his left foot to gain enough ground to keep his barrage of attacks coming. Joni's eyes, calm and cool, widened as he barely blocked each attempt to take control of the center. Unable to focus on each block *and* his own footing, Joni was forced backward.

Pirates shuffled out of his way as Joni took his next two quick steps to replant his feet. Katzgoode baited again, what looked like the same series of attacks. Seeing the familiar threat, Joni readied a counterattack. After he parried the same upper strike, he didn't expect a flying boot to kick him hard in the gut.

The failure to block came with adrenaline, ignoring the chance to catch his breath. Next came the killing blow. As his back heel pressed up against the taffrail, Joni pushed forward, dodging right as the blade neared his face. Using the strength of his legs, Joni propelled his body up against Katzgoode. Feet repositioned as the blades pressed up against each other, shaking to hold back each desire to kill, and to live.

Katzgoode stepped sideways while trying to trip Joni. Joni pulled back, giving Katzgoode his space before he began his own attacks. Quick and well placed, Joni didn't intend to lose the new advantage given. Each time Katzgoode tried to rediscover his footing, he felt the impact of each attack, resulting in sloppy reactions.

Joni softened his stance but Katzgoode, still stiff, looked for the opportunity to defend the attack his natural reaction told him was coming. None came. With his sword lowered and his stance open, Joni walked calmly toward his old captain. Katzgoode pulled back to lunge forward. With a sidestep and a straight-forward jab, the tip of Joni's blade entered Katzgoode's chest, stopping his sword hand from advancing. The lunge did all the work, pushing the sharp end into his own flesh. Katzgoode's attack was stuck, his arm could no longer move. The sword dropped, making a clatter that shook the captives to their core.

Katzgoode groaned in pain, then shouted in failure. When Joni pulled his blade back, blood filled the hole it just created, soaking up the fabric around it. Looking down in disbelief, he saw the dark red slowly grow next to his pendants. Doubling over, he saw not one face express love or respect, just pity and disappointment.

"Finish him off," Skye said.

Steely, Joni swiped, letting the last inch of his sword drag quickly across Katzgoode's throat. Skye laid his hand on Joni's shoulder.

"Atta boy, lad," Skye said before he whispered soft enough so only Joni could hear. "It gets easier, I promise."

Embracing the emotions, Joni only nodded. The pirates cheered while some received coin from placed bets.

"Oui, Joni? What say you regarding the rest of these sorry sacks?" Skye said as he walked up to his prisoners.

"My offer still stands one more time." Joni raised his hilt to point his bloody tip toward Pip.

"*Joni the Merciful.* Looks like you all got one more chance." Skye kicked the sword that was just dropped by Katzgoode in Pip's direction.

Pip looking around eventually bent down to pick up the weapon. Eyeing Joni, he wished he could erase the insults from time itself. Taking the stance, his eyes drifted until they landed on Katzgoode's corpse.

"Joni boy, you discredited the late captain, don't let that be your downfall this time," Skye said.
"Trust me Captain, I know." Joni squinted, held his stance more firmly and slowly edged his way toward Pip.
Pip raised his sword, placed his feet properly and dropped his blade and fell to his knees.
"Please, Joni Sir, don't strike me down. I swear it, you are indeed merciful even though I don't deserve any mercy, but I do beg of it," Pip cried out.

Like a toddler who found his fingers stuck in a door jam, his sobs were unlike anything these men had ever seen. Some laughed while others were disgusted by such cowardice. Even his own men found themselves embarrassed. Joni looked at Skye, questioning this unexpected display.

"You're making me sick you sorry excuse of a sailor. Get up!" Skye shouted. "You ever hear the term, *die with dignity?*"

Shuddering gasps of air were all Skye got as a response.

"I've never seen such lowly behavior, Sir. We ought to put him in the brig with the rest of these men. Let him wallow, surrounded by those who once served under him."

Joni came close enough to Skye to whisper. "We might have some use for such a weak man."

Skye's eyebrow rose in acceptance.

"You heard him. Bring these men down to the brig until we find what torturous fate awaits them," Skye barked. "Which reminds me, I have some new friends still down there."

* * * * *

"Rifi, Kagu, you can come out now," Kara whispered loudly.

The lily elf and goblin emerged from the darkness, looking to make sure they were alone.

"What is going on here?" Rifi asked, confused.

"Looks like they're pirating this ship from the inside," Marx said. "Skye mentioned this taking a year of planning. Not bad a return, considering how much this ship is worth in pay and weaponry. The cannons alone can hold an entire village hostage. What are *you guys* doing here?"

"We were just concerned for our good friends here, Kara and Ethen and it appears we were right to be concerned. In the short time away from the harbor, they were put in this smelly cage on a ship captured by pirates," Rifi said defensively.

"I was just accompanying our *new friend* here," Kara said before sharing a look with Marx to go along.

"Just stop it!" Ethen said. "We all know that you came here to steal that item Marx has. I'm tired of the lies. Rifi, Marx is a good man, and we want out of the thieves' life. We got turned down by the army, so Marx agreed to train me and help Kara sell her songs."

"Item? What item?" Rifi said.

"He's right Rifi, Marx already knows everything about the plot against him," Kara said. "We told him, and we found a way out. Reason why we're here in this smelly cage. But Ethen's right. We *are* sick of stealing and Marx has proven himself to be a good man. Something I'm not sure you even know exists."

Rifi spoke softly, seemingly to himself. "I do know it. That it leads to rumbling bellies."

"Look, Master Rifi, you or those who are offering you payment, have no idea what could happen if that item fell into the wrong hands. I cannot allow that to happen," Marx said.

"What item?" Elet asked.

"I'm sorry Elet. You must believe me when I say the less you know, the safer you are. You aren't the only one with secrets," Marx said.

"So, Rifi, will you help us? You could join, leave the life and become something much better. You can start by letting us out of this cell." Kara tapped the lock with her finger. "I know you could free us within seconds."

Rifi took a moment. "Or... I could go introduce myself to the new captain and let him in on the spoils."

Marx laughed. "By all means, feel free. You know what happened to the last men who tried to take it from me? All that will accomplish is letting me know where your allegiances lie." Marx sat against the wall and lowered his head. "In the end, it really makes no difference to me."

Rifi smiled as he walked up to the cell. "You must be decent gambler with a bluff like that." He brought his hands to the lock. "But not a bluff I'm willing meet. You sure did put a number on those guys." The lock clicked and the cell door sprung open. "Now, what's the plan?"

"I appreciate you letting us free and showing which side you're on. However, it appears that I already found favor with the new captain and am curious where that'll lead. I don't see the point of letting us out quite yet. Unless we intend to overtake the ship ourselves. Seems unnecessary. So, I think it's best we discuss our plan together."

"Skye intends to take us to Rimcaster, the southern trading station. It's outside common law and therefore, unpredictable. I *need* to go north," Elet said.

"Assuming Skye keeps his word, can you afford a week's time?" Marx asked. "Keep in mind the question: what choice do we have?"

Elet sighed. "I can afford a week but not much longer."

"Also, I don't think Skye was just interested in your gold. He needed you for this plan to work. There's no way he could have assumed that they wouldn't just sink his boat. Notice he asked us to tie him up and surrender before the ship caught up to us. As if that was his plan from the start."

Elet's eyes squinted at the idea that she was a piece of a game she never agreed to playing.

"What good will that do us now?" she puffed.

"Alone, probably nothing now but any information is useful information. Skye also finds favor in those under him and part of the reason he was able to pull off this heist is not just loyalty but understanding the value in men and information. I think he may have found that value in me. Bringing that piece into light, I think him trusting me might be within our benefit."

"Trust, huh?" Rifi questioned. "Using trust as a means of leverage, hmm. I thought you were supposed to be a good man."

"I'm not even sure what is meant by the word good, let alone if I meet the standard. But yes, leverage is always a tool to take into consideration, and no, I don't plan to betray his trust. Not if I don't have to. I have an inkling he's not so bad." Marx twisted his neck and stretched back his shoulders. "The question is do we reveal you and your friend? That will be up to you. Just know, we're friends now. Don't betray that trust and I will do what I can to keep you and your friend safe." Marx curled comfortably against the wall as he got ready to wait.

"What's up with Kagu anyways? He's really quiet," Kara said.

"I have on me a freshly dead lizard that Kagu will get all to himself if he remains quiet. He's really good at making deals," Rifi said with a wink. Kagu smiled as the master of trades in his own mind.

"I think you should stay hidden, just in case these guys aren't as good as Marx assumes," Elet said.

"Yeah, you should stay hidden. Just in case." Kara echoed before she shut the unlocked door.

"As much as I want to decline due to the smell alone, I'm not so sure they'll take a liking to you-know-who." Rifi shifted his eyes toward Kagu.

Kagu looked back. "Me no who?"

Several sets of feet strummed the stairs. Skye appeared first, wearing his new attire. He strutted his steps toward the cell. Marx waited until he halted before standing up to greet the new captain.

"Aye, I haven't forgotten about you. Sorry you had to endure the stench. I typically think such treatment is *untasteful*. However, with the brig's *new* guests, I see a point of sharing the irony. Now, before I swap bodies, can I trust you?" Skye asked Marx, dropping his smile.

Marx stood and walked toward the cell door. "You can."

"How can I be so sure?"

Marx pressed his finger against the door that slowly opened.

"I suppose you can't really, but we have no reason to cross you. Or do we?" Marx met Skye's striking blue eyes with a minigame of Don't Blink.

Skye bellowed with laughter.

"I knew you were all right people. So, missy, you still sore at me?" Skye asked Elet.

"I was just a part of your plan to take over this ship. I do not like being taken advantage of *Captain*," Elet said, holding firm her stance.

"An improvised part of my plan, but you're right missy. I will get you up north free of charge for playing your part. I find no pleasure in cheating those who have assisted me and my crew. Unless they have no idea they took part," Syke snickered. "I'm pleased to know you're quick enough to put two and two together. I believe you'll fit right in."

Skye happily flung open the door and bowed while Marx, Elet, Kara, and Ethen exited past him. They were replaced with Pip and the other men.

"Let's get you up to some fresh air and I'll discuss with what the next few days will look like," Skye said.

"Don't forget us!" Rifi said as he popped out of the darkness with a pinched nose, Kagu behind him. "I'd love in on that fresh air too."

Startled, swords flashed toward the small elf. Rifi raised his arms.

"Sorry, we snuck on board at Laneloon to help save our friends here," Rifi pointed to the young siblings. "We assumed they were coming back to the harbor. Nice work on pirating this fine ship by the way, Captain, Skye is it?"

"You knew they were there?" Skye's direction went to Marx.

"I did. Just as you didn't find it necessary to tell Miss Elet your plans, I didn't find it necessary to tell you mine," Marx said. "However, I didn't keep it a secret due to any part of my own concern but of my lily elf's friend there. As you know, most kill them on the spot, but I assure you, he is different than any other goblin."

With Rifi's hands raised, he left his satchel unprotected. Kagu was finally free to snatch the dead lizard for himself. In an instant he shoved it in his mouth. He turned to see all eyes on him. He stared back, confused, with the dead lizard's tail stuck out of his mouth.

Chapter Seven
Symbols & god Talk

"I heard about these cannon thingies. Another crazy invention gone right by those gnomes, huh?" Rifi said as they passed the Gun Deck.

Kork shot the lily elf a stern stare.

"Crazy good, of course," Rifi added.

"That's nothing compared to what we got cooking back at the homeland: Tinker's Ticker. We've had these cannon prints stashed in the vault for at least two hundred years. So, we shared them for needed parts. We figured something as simple as shoving a ball down a tube with the mixture of charcoal, sulfur, and potassium nitrate was something children could figure out. Still, I shouldn't give humans that much credit. Even if it's elementary."

"You didn't think through the harm it'd do. We are talking about humans after all." Rifi looked back to the humans behind him. "No offense."

"We figured it might as well be in human hands, rather than o'rüks. No elf cares for destruction tools and no dwarf has the humility to admit we got something worth bartering. Although, the way humans have been acting nowadays, I'm not so sure," Kork said.

"You sure you gnomes sold it to the right humans?" Kara asked.

"No, we're not," Kork replied. "But we're excited to see the results. It might just teach us something new."

"You keep saying '*we*'. You still keep in contact with your kind, being so far away and all?" Rifi asked.

"I return home every twenty or so years and I write them every couple. Plus, we have a slice of our family close. You'll meet them soon enough. They keep in touch more than I," Kork said.

"What other kind of inventions you got cooking?" Rifi pressed.

"Never mind that, *elf*. I thought your kind doesn't meddle in the discoveries of science. Although, I've never seen your kind in the company with a gob before either. Which *is* curious within itself," Kork replied as they reached the main deck, catching up with Skye and the rest.

"So, what is our plan, *Captain?*" Elet asked, bitterness stuck in her throat.

"You still cross with me?" Skye stopped pacing to face her. "Look, I am the captain, and I have been playing nice. I will make it up to you, missy, or I won't. Getting on my bad side isn't going to work out for you or your friends. Understand?" Skye froze for her response.

She blinked first. "I suppose you're right. I apologize. So, does that mean you will help me get back north?"

"Keep it friendly and you have my word."

"What's at Rimcaster?" Marx asked.

"We're actually going to an island close to there. I need to return that boat and then I will make sure you can catch a ride up the strait with one of the trade ships. It won't be a problem, and you'll be safe; I assure you. Assuming trades go as planned, I'll even throw in a little for your trouble."

"I'm sure we appreciate it," Marx said.

"Here are your belongings," Skye gestured to Elet's baggage, bow and the others' weapons. Before Marx had a chance to grab his blade, Skye snatched it up. He studied the longer hilt to blade ratio. "Never seen a blade alike. I imagine leverage is the idea."

Marx nodded.

"Never a bad thing to have, that's for sure. Maybe one day you can show me how you use it. Which reminds me, after your business is concluded with missy here, how would you like working for me?"

"I am not certain. I also have long-term business with these two young siblings here," Marx said.

"Very good." Skye handed Marx his weapon. "I wouldn't want you to decide so quickly anyhow. There's plenty of nights for you to sleep on it."

"I'll take you up on that offer, to sleep that is. I haven't slept well in many nights, since before the storm. Where can we stay?" Marx said.

"Phin, you were about to go down to rest yourself, no? Please show our guests to the stateroom. Missy, you can sleep in the captain's quarters," Skye said with a smile.

"Is *that* what you mean by 'play nice'? You might as well throw me overboard right now," Elet puffed.

Skye laughed. "You're a vibrant flower, that's for true, but that's not what I meant. I sleep more comfortably in the crow's nest, alone with the stars."

"Oh, well, I'm sorry. I didn't know," Elet said.

"It's fine, missy. Those in the brig had their own quarters down in the galley. I'm sure you'll find the beds cozy. It's across the way from the captain's cabin," Skye said.

"Are you sure? You or your men won't want to sleep in them?" Marx asked.

"The crew sleeps better in swinging hammocks, and the new mates need to roughen up a bit. Trust me," Skye assured. "You need anything else, please address Joni here."

Joni stepped forward.

"Again, thank you Captain," Marx said.

"You sure got those bullies back." Kara said.

"Payback wasn't the plan. But it did help things along. I wasn't the only one treated poorly," Joni said with a grin.

"Serves those jerks right." Kara returned the smile.

"Yes, thank you, Captain. Sorry I've been cross," Elet said.

"Old storms missy. The captain's cabin is straight that way."

"Um, Elet?" Kara asked.

"Yes, dear?"

"Would you mind sleeping in the same room as us? I would just feel more comfortable with you around," Kara said with soft eyes.

Elet looked to Marx who shrugged before asking Kara: "You sure?"

A split second and Kara shot him a glance. Marx understood her concern: the safety of his necklace.

"I suppose I could." Elet said.

"Marx, go ahead and take the captain's cabin. You deserve it," Kara said. "He's helped us a lot."

"Um, sure. He actually helped *me* quite a bit too." Elet admitted.

"Isn't he the best?" Kara said.

Now it was Marx who shot Kara a look as if to say, *not so thick*. His face returned when Elet eyed him.

"Are you sure? I feel guilty. You are a lady, after all. Give the word, and the cabin is yours."

"I don't mind at all. Again, girl's time is appreciated."

After it was decided they turned to see a patient Phin waiting. He took the lead toward the back of the ship, past the galley and to the back to the stateroom. Looking in, the room was much nicer than the rest. The four beds looked a lot more comfortable than the torn-up hammocks.

"This will certainly do. Thank you, Phin," Elet said.

"Not a worry ma'am. Um, you sure he is containable?" Phin asked Rifi. "You know we're taking a risk not keeping him in the brig."

"I assure you, he isn't dangerous. Just ask any of them," Rifi said.

"He's not like any other goblin," Kara said.

"She's right. I swear it," Ethen agreed.

"I, too, was concerned when I first saw him. But he has shown kindness that I've never seen his kind display before," Marx added.

Phin's eyes finally landed on Elet.

"Don't look at me. I've never seen him before the brig." Elet said dismissively. "I was kind of glad you brought it up." She caught sight of Ethen and Kara's pleading eyes. "However, if my new friends here trust him, so do I."

"Well, the votes are unanimous. Sleep tight," Phin said as he walked away.

"Good night, Marx. Sorry I've been so moody, but all things considered…" Elet said.

"No need to apologize. I completely understand, *all things considered*. This isn't what any of us expected. But I'd be lying to say I'm not enjoying myself. Now I can say I have been involved in a pirate's heist and scratch that off my list of insane things done. How about you? Are you okay? Truly?"

"If I took pages out of your book, I can't imagine I'd ever be sore in any situation. I'm glad I had the chance to see you again, Marx," Elet smiled one last time before turning away for the night.

"Please yell if you need me," Marx said as she waved, her head still turned away.

"Night Marx," the siblings said together, Kara making a kissy face; Ethen laughed.

"Goodnight you two," Marx replied shaking his head. "Night master Rifi, Sir Kagu."

"Me not Sir, me goblin," Kagu said.

"Night mister Marx," Rifi said pulling Kagu to follow him.

Before he was given access to the captain's cabin, about a half a dozen of Skye's men were on their way out carrying everything from maps to half drunken liquor bottles, leaving nothing behind but naked furniture. Once inside, Marx placed a wooden wedge under the door, keeping it from opening from the outside in. He was happy to shed his travel-worn cloak and his once soft silks that were now hardened from dried sweat. The stench filled his lungs which he wasn't proud to claim as his own.

The captain's cabin was twice the size of the room he had slept in at the Barrel. This didn't include another section that was large enough to fit a king-sized bed, large dressers, on either side and a walk-in closest. The comparison to the six-foot crow's nest Skye preferred added a layer of admiration for the new captain.

The sheets, pillows, blankets, and mattress were pulled off of its frame. *It appears pirates don't believe in leaving any stone unturned*, Marx thought. Still, he couldn't remember a time he was treated with such hospitality. Putting the bed back together, he felt guilty, thinking how much more comfortable this bed was than the wet ground he'd grown used to.

He pulled out the necklace, not sure if he wanted anymore. With all the trouble it could cause, he thought about throwing it out the cabin's window and letting it sink to the bottom of the ocean. However, he knew his duty and how dire it was that he fulfill it. He cursed himself for engaging with those mercenaries merely for the fact he knew he'd win. He humbly admitted his human condition in a prayer and found favor in forgiveness, both from the gods and for himself, putting the thought out of his mind.

He cut one long piece of fabric from his silk shirt to tie tight around his inner thigh. There, it would be unlikely anyone could pickpocket the necklace. Once he put back on his shorts and buried himself in the covers, he figured it was finally time to catch up on his journal. He pulled out a pen that he found on one of the men who tried to ambush him. He figured it was fair payment for the trouble; they weren't likely to get a better deal from any other person they'd tried to rob.

He scooted one of the dressers so he could set up his ink as he lit his candle. In place and ready to write he thought about everything that had gone on since he last wrote. Reading what he last wrote he was surprised at what had happened since. His head sunk into the goose-down pillow. Before jotting the first letter, he figured it was fine to close his eyes, for just a moment's time.

*   *   *   *   *

The violent storm shook the forest as far as it stretched, causing trees and their branches to sway to the point of cracking. Winds blew with such force Marx expected the trees to uproot and fly into the chaos above. The red sky flared, flickering, nearly as a constant. All he could hope for was the little strength left in his legs would allow him to continue. A small building lay up ahead. Explosions of light continued to blast above him. Finding just enough will to defy the storm, he bolted, reaching the building as the ground broke, crumbling apart beneath his last step.

He slammed the door behind him and as he did, the maddening sound stopped. A window revealed the forest was calm and unmoving. The room was pitched in black. Strangely, the dazzling light didn't find its way in. A table was revealed by an appearing flame floating atop of it.

Walking up, he felt the candle's black neck and beside it, a vase holding a sunflower. The yellow petals shined brightly in contrast to the dark background. The black center of the flower was melded with the darkness, giving the impression that the petals, like the flame, floated in the void. With a closer look the petals were beige, not yellow. The flower was dead.

The clear vase shimmered dimly, then glowed a little brighter, clear blue, or was the water within it? The lit water rose slowly until it reached the brim and spilled over. Picking it up, he saw no water enter, yet it somehow overflowed onto his hands. Setting it back down, the glowing blue liquid now gushed out forcing the dead sunflower out. It splashed onto and off the table, knocking the candle over and dousing the flame.

Only the water produced a faint light as it quickly covered the floor. Soon, his feet were submerged. Not sure what to do, he ran to the door. It didn't budge. Going to the window, he no longer saw a forest but an open sea. Large waves curved up over Marx's view outside before their tops blew away from high winds.

Panic set in when the water inside rose up to his ribcage. He hit the window, figuring he'd escape. The first strikes did nothing. With one more chance, he took a deep breath, tightened his fist and wailed once more. The window cracked and when it did, the weight from the waves outside pressed against the glass until it caved and shattered.

Whether the building sank into the ocean or the water from outside rose over it, Marx couldn't tell. The room was filled either way. Trapped inside the room, forcefully dragged below, his throat tightened at the thought: that the last breath of air was gone ages ago. He wondered how much longer he could last. Blurred, a sea serpent came into view. It watched just out of reach. The reptilian face was smooth, wise yet almost mocked Marx as he slowly drowned. His only hope, his last hope was that this was all just a bad dream. Wait, he thought!

Marx woke up gasping. Looking around, then to the window, he saw Lux, still shimmering off the black ocean surface. The candle's wax suggested he was sleeping no more than an hour. His journal was opened and lay at his side. He flipped to the back where he jotted notes.

Sunflower, candle, vase with overflowing water (blue glow). Trapped in small room. I was in a forest then sea. Storms. Drowned. Sea Serpent.

What do sunflowers represent, he wondered as he stared at the words. The first thing that came to mind was Elet and her yellow dress. Perhaps the candle represented Skye. His red feather symbolized the flame, the flame's bottom blue his eyes. Then the water, overflowing from the vase, eventually filling up the room and drowning him. The serpent watched, uncaring.

These damn dreams. It seemed every time peace tried to find its way within him, these dreams turned it away at the door. He wished he could dismiss them, rewrap himself in the quilts and go back to sleep. Yet, he couldn't shake the desperation he felt moments ago. If the dream was a warning, he should at least warn the captain.

He threw on his pants and shirt, unwedged the door, and walked out. Spilled dice and laughter came from the pirates still awake on the other side of stateroom. He peered in to check on Elet and the siblings. The lantern's last light fought to provide just enough to see bodies in the beds. He'd let them rest. Climbing the stairs, he ran into a pair of pirates at the top who took notice.

"You lost?" one said.

"No, I would like a word with the captain. Is he up in the crow's nest?" Marx asked.

"Nah. He's at the bow. I'll take ya to 'em," the other pirate said suspiciously, turning as he led the way.

They saw Skye and Kork facing the sea ahead.

"Ahem, Sir. You have a visitor."

"Ah, Marx. At ease chaps," Skye said. "What can I do you for? Bed too soft?"

"Unlike you, I don't have that problem. The bed is the most comfortable one I've slept in in years if not my life; I drifted immediately.

"I wanted to first ask. You mentioned the gods. That was before I knew your plans to take this ship. Do you truly follow them?" Marx asked.

"Hah! Which ones? Seems more are being born each new day. Laying laws to collect coin or build armies. I reckon the gods anew are all selling the same charlatan's brew."

"So, you don't follow them?"

"I never said I followed them. I yield to them if it serves me right. But yes, I *do* believe. I've met one."

Marx raised a brow. "You have? And who is that?"

"Guagala, god of the sea."

"Is that another newly birthed? Never heard of her."

"That's because she stays concealed. Why all this talk about gods anyways? What are you gettin' at?"

"Although I side with your beliefs about the new gods, mortal crafted to fit mortal aims, I'm sure, I wondered if you believe in things *unseen*."

"What? Like ghosts, or the afterlife?"

"I mean meaning or purpose from, for lack of a proper word, the *unknown*. Like a calling to the sea or, a warning. This may sound foolish and maybe it is. But I just had a dream, and I fear it may be that kind of warning. In it I drowned. I don't know how but since you're the captain, I figured I'd let you know, to take heed."

"Do *you* believe in the gods?" Skye asked.

"Only the ones that matter," Marx replied.

"And who are those?"

"Nih and Nil."

"The twins. It's well-believed Nil is no longer with us."

"To me, she is still divine, even if she doesn't dwell among us any longer," Marx said.

"And isn't Nih the god of the elves?" Skye asked.

Kork spoke up. "She sure is. Nih abandoned the world centuries ago."

"Did you ever think that it was the world that had abandoned him? That maybe the elves still have that relationship because they're the only ones who care?" Marx asked.

"No, I hadn't given that a thought. But if that's the case, the elves abandoned the world too and they can have each other for all I care. Not that us gnomes have ever cared about the gods," Kork replied.

"Once you did."

"That was a long time ago, well before the new age."

Skye looked at Marx up and down.

"No offense, holy man, but if I addressed every bad dream, I'd be chasing shadow men under every child's bed for a livin. Dreams are nothing but disorganized thoughts. They bear no consequence to the real world. How bout you pray to your elf god, and I'll keep a sharp lookout, as I always do. I wouldn't lose sleep over it," Skye said.

"In this instance, I hope you're right. Thanks for the discussion." Marx turned. "Good night."

Marx made his way back down to the captain's cabin, curious about this sea god, Guagala. Skye spoke plainly of her. More so, he claimed to have met her. *Why would he lie?* Stripping off his crusty clothes once more, he knelt, whispered a prayer to Nih, and fell back asleep.

Chapter Eight
The Last Southern Island

The sun rose, crossed the sky, and disappeared two times before it rose one last time as the ship neared its arrival. Within those long days, Ethen and Marx spent much of that time at the stern, going over combat fundamentals. Marx was impressed with Ethen's persistence, always found outside his room each morning. While they trained, Kara and Elet shared pieces of their past.

Marx often watched the three from afar, smiles on their faces. Elet grew more beautiful each passing day, a feat which seemed impossible. Marx's rogue life always found a way to dodge what caught many by surprise,—a road to a family. A mystery before, why anyone would choose to abandon the thrill of adventure, now started to make sense.

The first night, Kara entertained the pirates with her songs. The second night, many memorized most of the words as they sang and stomped the main deck. Marx would reinforce the idea that her claim to success was just a matter of time. The challenge, he teased, would be keeping the crowds off her. Still, she played the skeptic, even if a shade of blush rose with the thought. Just as a shade of blush rose when Joni gave her praise, a spark Marx knew enough to tease.

Rifi and Kagu fit right in with the pirates and their conduct. With enough answered questions, Rifi admitted that the pirates had benefits that the thieves did not. For one, the code to share the spoils and to live as one. This suppressed the tactic to lie to one another, and with their eyes on much bigger prizes, it also offset the constant hustle.

Skye and his men also took a particular liking to Kagu. The goblin provided entertainment for the men. They admired his unique kindness, as far as goblins go. They were also fond of his bluntness, calling it *gob-logic*. A joke at first, his simple responses were never too far from what rang true. What men felt necessary to complicate, Kagu's showed life isn't all that complicated, at least for pirates anyway.

"Who knew what we've been missing this entire time, a lily elf and goblin duo," Skye admitted jokingly. "Join our ranks if ya want. We can make it official. An initiation back at the Nest."

Marx was up well before the sun. Peeking outside his door and finding no sign of Ethen, he figured he'd take the time to meditate in prayer. Two or so hours later, the sun barely lit up his room. Still, with no sign of Ethen, he decided to join those on the main deck. He peeked into the stateroom, finding it empty.

Overcast fought the sun which faintly covered the ship with gloomy shades of gray. The strong scent of seaweed clung to the foggy mist. Emerging from below, Marx found his company near the bow with Skye, Kork and a few pirates.

"You're up early," Marx said to his friends.

"We're just excited to get off this ship," Kara said. "Not sure how they do it."

"How far is Rimcaster?" Marx asked Skye who stood at the tip of the bow staring out ahead.

"We passed it just before dawn. Lucky too, as this fog assured no one saw us pass. Although folks there are decent at keeping our business out of govies' ears, they *aren't* as decent as refusing gossip." Skye never shifted his gaze as he spoke.

"How'd you sleep?" Elet asked Marx.

"I'm afraid I'll never get a chance to sleep that well again. And for that, I'm glad to no longer have the temptation." Marx smiled with hopes he would see her smile back. Something he grew fonder of each day. The daily prize was given. "How about you?"

"Oh, we slept well enough. Although Ethen wouldn't stop talking about the different openings you taught him. You created quite the little monster," Elet said playfully.

"Sorry to keep you up," Ethen said.

"It's okay, I'm encouraged by your ambition. Wish I had that same drive at your age."

"Isn't that the truth," Marx agreed.

"If it isn't the great and powerful Phin. I thought you were dead down there," Kork yelled at the wizard's appearance, first they've seen since he first went down.

"A wizard never has enough time to study; such is our curse. Not that I could study much with all you buffoons stomping the main deck practically to splinters," Phin said.

"Joni boy, go adjust the sails. Twenty degrees starboard," Skye ordered as he left the bow to take over the helm.

Joni went to the center of the main deck, yelling orders. Skye switched places with one of the helmsmen. A moment later and the ship obeyed the helm's wheel.

"How'd he know to turn?" Ethen asked. "I can't see anything."

Soon the haze on their right grew dark. A sudden land mass towered over them.

"Reef the sails!" Skye yelled as others repeated the order all the way to Joni. "Drop anchor!"

The ship slowed as the island came nearer. The sun broke free, lighting up the land. White sand and clear turquoise water breathed life into the dull, dead morning. A single steep mountain, covered in tropical trees rose over them until its peak was lost in the hazy sky up above.

"It's beautiful," Elet said.

Random bungalows protruded out of the vegetation throughout. Water fell from the hidden mountaintop overhead, filling large buckets causing them to dip. The buckets rotated around a vertical conveyer belt lifting the other side up—platforms mounted on the bucket's bottom. Large gears, about ten feet in diameter, on either side were attached to smaller gears as they turned together. A large metal cylinder rattled, whistled, and released a cloud of steam every so often. The siblings were bouncing around the main deck

"What in the world is that?" Kara pointed here.

"And what are those?" Ethen pointed over there.

"Some of those crazy inventions gone right," Kork replied, eyeing Rifi.

"Not bad Korky, not bad at all. Umm what *do* those things do anyways?" Rifi asked

"Never mind elf. Not that you'd understand if I told you," Kork said.

"Welcome to Filong Underbelly. Last island before the icy lands of Stellich. It's pretty much forgotten or unknown to the rest of the world. Too far south and always covered in fog, no one bothers us here. And if they did, this island is more than capable of defending itself. With help from our smaller friends here," Skye said giving Kork a push.

"Just keep steering," Kork said as he lit an end of a pointed tube and held it over his head. "I'll let them know it's us."

The tube flew out of his hand and exploded over the ship, shooting sparks abroad, high-pitched whistles sang as they did.

"I don't see a dock up ahead," Elet pointed out.

"Docks gets in our way." Kork pointed.

On shore, a stack of wooden planks, with a transferable wire on each side, unfolded. It grew until its last piece landed in place as the gangway, just as the ship stopped suddenly, as if something grabbed it from the bottom. Everyone instinctively used a planted foot, preventing themselves from falling over.

"Guests first. Can somebody help the lady," Skye said.

"I'll assist," Marx said.

"And what about you two?" Skye asked Rifi and Kagu. "Why don't you get off here. Our shorter friends would love to meet you, according to your unique friendship. I'll send for you tonight. To get your answer to join us."

"Aye, captain." Rifi's eyes never left the strange contraptions on shore.

"Ah, there's Bell. She's a doll and she'll be happy to treat anything she's capable." Skye waved before shoeing Elet and rest along, no pirate followed. "Actually, Marx. Would you mind joining me once you're done with those bags?"

"Sure. As long as it's okay with Elet," Marx said.

Scanning the island, she saw gnomes and a few humans. Considering their height and friendly faces, she nodded. More gnomes spilled from the bungalows to greet the ship. A female gnome with large, kind eyes, brown and white hair tied up in a knot ran up to happily introduce herself.

"Wow, look at that! A full rigger. Ooh, *ana* new faces. Ello, name's Bell, at your service. Welcome to Filong Underbelly. Please, follow me," Bell said as she curtsied and shook each of their hands, stopping and Kagu. "Oh my! How are you, good sir? And you are?"

"Me Goblin," Kagu said.

"That's Kagu," Rifi answered.

"Okay, dear, truly stunning to have you here. So many questions. As you may know, we love questions." Bell turned, and scurried ahead.

She led them to the series of rope ladders.

"Please, leave your luggage here. I'd first like to show you around. It's not often we get new visitors," Bell said.

"You sure you're okay?" Marx asked Elet.

She giggled. "I think I can manage. Go. Just be back by nightfall, if you wish that is. I think we may go for a swim after the tour. What do you think?" she asked the siblings who agreed.

"You coming?" Bell asked before she turned back around and went ahead.

She pulled a rope ladder before she slid it under one of the elevating platforms to hook one. "You got to be quick here. Grab hold when it rises."

Bell was lifted up. Kara and Ethen gleefully joined before the rest followed. They were lifted through several stories before they disappeared from Marx's sight.

Marx wished he could join them. Although, he *was* curious what Skye wanted to show him. He saw some of the crew carrying boxes and other goods that belonged to the ship off of it. Skye, Kork, and Phin stood at the stern.

"I need to get back to my studies. I'm very close to mastering a spell," Phin said.

"What kind of spell?" Skye asked.

"A complex one," Phin returned.

"You won't tell me?" Skye pushed.

"I will if I can pull it off, how's that?" Phin passed Marx and exited the gangway.

"Deal," Skye said, noticing Marx. "Ah, got away from the missy. I'm afraid she'll never let you go once your business is concluded, eh?"

Marx flushed.

"I'm just kiddin ya. I wanted to show you my nest on *my* side of the island," Skye said.

"Your side?" Marx asked

"Aye, it's a little rough around the edges. Figured it'd be best for the youngens and your pretty friend if they'd stay with the gnomes. They love to have guests."

"Phin doesn't stay with you?"

"Nah. He prefers the minds of the little know-it-alls. Not to mention the quiet. My boys tend to drink when they sing; until the sun rises."

Marx had to agree with Phin's take. Looking at the back of the ship, *The Path of Righteousness* was towed behind it. He saw the gnomes happily collecting random pieces of metal on board.

"Payment," Skye answered. "We provide metal, the weirder the better, and they provide the island's safety, gnome plans and food once and a while. Not that it always tastes good. They aren't always spot on with their inventions. So, you ready?"

Skye waved his arms and a moment later the ship, its sails still full, moved forward as something underneath let it go. Around the bend up ahead the ship turned right, sharp, into a cove. Three other ships docked on shore, none as large as the new ship they rode. Beyond that, several ship wreckages came together into the cove's corner.

"Those are the poor souls who weren't invited here," Skye pointed out. "The gnomes aren't the only protection we have."

"What other protection do you have?" Marx asked.

Skye ignored him. Something besides the helm started steering the ship until it docked itself.

"Magic?" Marx asked.

"Nope. We have a system under us. A grid of ropes that hook us from under," Kork advised.

"Boys! We're home!" Skye yelled loud enough for all to hear. "Now go enjoy yourselves. That's an order. You've earned it. And you, newly recruited. Welcome yourselves, we have plenty of rooms, food, and liquor."

The pirates cheered, announcing to the other pirates on shore who cheered back at the arrival of their mates and their new prize. As though they held back their pirate-like behavior until now, they each jumped off the ship and ran around the island hollering. Rum, wine and other liquors were handed out, tobacco and weeds were rolled and stuffed in pipes while campfires lit up and caught fish and wild hog were cooked.

"Let me show you around," Skye offered.

Getting a closer look, the shipwrecks were purposely placed, leveled and even inhabited. Looking up, walls of jagged rock held multiple wooden bridges hung high to the very top. Where bridges ended another wretched ship was made into a home.

"I'm not sure what's more fascinating, here or the gnome's side," Marx said, awed. "I've traveled around; this place is truly unique."

"Yeah, I like it too. The only land I don't mind staying at when away from the sea." Skye stopped to greet someone.

The pirate handed Skye a bottle. He snatched it up and took two large gulps and breathed out the fumes. He took the time to speak with his passing men during their climb among the bridges. *These men respected him*, Marx noticed. *More as a friend than a superior.* The beach below shrunk as they finally reached the peak. Skye stopped at a small hut, a tall pole sticking out of its roof. Marx wasn't surprised to see a crow's nest at the top.

"I assume this one's yours. Nice touch," Marx admitted.

"Thanks."

"What is it you enjoy about the stars? Aside from their beauty that is," Marx said.

"I enjoy the feeling of being separated from this world. Like the sea, the stars represent a clean slate of new beginnings and untold adventures. You know, the tribe I'm from, we believed the stars are passed on, loved ones." Marx saw Skye's blues shimmer, a concealed shade of sadness.

"What tribe are you from?" Marx asked.

"A forgotten one," Skye answered.

Marx should have known not to ask. Still, he was interested in Skye. His character, his acquired shipmates and gnome friends, and now more than ever, his past. *The stars are his fallen, loved once;* Marx put the rest together; he finds comfort close to those who are no longer with him.

"I'm sorry."

"Don't be. Do you know why I like you, Marx? Most those men down there, I'm not sure they'd respect me without a reason to. Back there, you showed your values and never asked anything in return. Men like that are hard to come by. Trust me, this has become my life's work. I'm not in this business for the booty but for those I can trust. Trust to help me change the world. You follow Nih, and from what I know of him, he is a god of peace. Which means you know there's something terribly wrong with the world and it's getting worse by the day."

"I thought I was the only one who noticed. I feel it too. Especially as of late."

"Maybe you're the only one who admits it."

"Maybe. Or maybe no one's willing to say anything out loud. How do you suppose you'll fix the world's problems?" Marx asked.

Skye laughed. "I have no idea but what I *do* know it starts with loyalty. The gold I acquire, I give it all back to those men down there, trying desperately to believe that I can depend on them when it matters. But I'm not so sure, for the fact that it takes the gold in the first place. Would those men still follow me if I gave them nothing? All I can trust are Kork and Phin. They've been with me from the beginning, before anyone called me Captain.

"I've known Kork the longest, since I was a young lad. He doesn't understand humans and although gnomes love things they don't understand, he admits figuring us out is beyond even gnome comprehension.

"And Phin only trusts his magic that he says never betrays him, even if it takes most his time to understand it. I'm starting to wonder if I should have picked up magic instead, at least he has something he can trust, something that assures him why he's here. A purpose."

"I couldn't help but wonder about him. Wizards are quite unique. Aren't you afraid for his safety. I've heard what they do to those they find. Do you?" Marx asked.

"Torture them until they give up another wizard, spell book or magical item. They die from exhaustion, whether they give up everything or not."

"I never heard to that extreme."

"Trust me, I try to talk him out of it each chance I can. But he tells me that he can't express the rush and freedom his magic gives him. He compares it to my love of the sea. At the day's end, he's his own and I'm here to respect that. So, I choose to stay by his side and protect him to the death if need be. Plus, he is on his way to becoming quite powerful. Doesn't sound to me to be a bad thing, to have him on my side. Still, I worry about him."

"I know how you feel. I once had a friend in love with his magic," Marx said.

"Once?"

"He met his end. Don't worry, he wasn't captured, but it was tragic. He killed himself before he was taken alive. A common occurrence for magic user."

"Aye, Phin knows this. However, he refuses to entertain the idea. With the adventures we've had over the years, he says with me at his side, he'll more likely get eaten by a pack of parrots than get caught.

"So, what about you Marx? That blade and those clothes, you have a unique story yourself, I'm sure."

"I have a few tales."

"What is it you want to achieve in this vapor we call life?"

"Same as you, I suppose. However, I don't think us mortals can do much about it. So, I turn to the gods."

"Ah, so this is why you follow them? You keep saying *gods*, it was my understanding Nil is no longer a god. Why do you still consider her one?" Skye asked.

"I don't think gods can be stripped away of their divinity so easily. Or at least she still gets my praise. She gave up her power to bind Listar, to help each of us still here on Iris. I don't think people understand what she gave up for what we have today, let alone thankful for it."

"Maybe because they never heard that before. I never have. Well, not fully. There are many variations of the Twin's story. And it happened so long ago, I'm not sure it wasn't just made-up myths. Can you?"

"I can. When you meet a god, you know the truth is all there is. Or at least I used to think so. My encounter with Nih seems ages ago. Now, I'm not so sure my prayers are heard let alone answered." Marx never said that thought out loud. "You said you met a god yourself? What was her name?"

"Aye, Guagala," Skye answered.

"What's she like?"

"Very passive. She cares little about mortals and our squabbles. However, she assists me once and a while. She doesn't give me much of a reason to follow her or swear my allegiance or anything."

"How do you know she's truly a god?"

"I guess I don't. But she hasn't given me any reason not to trust her." Skye kicked open his hut's door.

A cat whined on his arrival.

"Smidgens! You crazy cat. Have you been waiting in here the whole time?" Skye bent over to scratch a fat orange cat behind the ear to the bottom of his tail. The cat's rear rose. "Don't know what this cat likes about me. I never even feed it. I enjoy the company, I must admit. Especially *because* I don't feed him. He likes me for who I am.

"Which brings me to you Marx. You appear to like me for who I am. You don't desire gold, and like me, you want to change the world for the better. Would you consider joining me one day?"

"I'm still not sure. However, I would be more than honored to call you a friend. That's not a no, just as it's not a yes. For now, let's just leave it at that."

"No tension here. I like that answer. It's honest." Skye smiled as he dropped some bags he'd been carrying. "And I'm glad to call you friend too."

He kicked off his heavy boots that clunked when they landed. "Ah, I hate these things. Phin talked me into wearing them for the new recruits. See what I mean? Appearances are sometimes worth more than the truth. What other lies must I entertain to convince these men to follow me?"

"Appearances? Like masquerading as an escort?" Marx challenged bluntly.

"Aye, precisely my point." Skye started digging through a few bags. "I'm more trapped as the captain than I am the free gull I desire to be. But to make a big difference, I suppose I must make big sacrifices. I *have* to believe it will be worth it. No one else seems to care enough to do anything about the twisted ways of the world."

"And what do you think that ship will achieve, exactly?" Marx asked.

"Nothin but a ripple," Skye said as he reached toward the bottom of a bag.

He pulled out a few smooth, round stones and shoved a few into his pockets.

"You wonder why I believe Guagala is a god?" Skye asked.

"Yeah?"

"You wanna meet her? I'm on my way to see her now."

Chapter Nine

Distrust to Embarrassed

"Follow me," Skye yelled as he dropped off the cliff.

With a post planted by Skye's hut, a pulley held by rope stretched down to the pirate's dock. Marx watched Skye fly and shook his head, looking down at the leather straps Skye had thrown at his feet.

It was hard to dismiss that Skye's character was growing on him. He thought what kind of luminous adventures they might have had in their younger years, or what possible adventures awaited their future. *Is this where fate was placing me?* he wondered. Just a flicker of Elet and he put the idea out of his head. Wrapping the leather around the rope, he flew down the intense drop, landing him back by the ships.

"Oui, Joni boy. Where is your bottle?" Skye asked.

"I'd rather wait until dusk, Sir," Joni replied.

"Don't like to drink in the light, eh? I can appreciate that. Come, I'm on my way to the other side of the cove. Care to join me?"

Joni looked off into the gloom afar and replied bravely. "Aye Sir."

Skye, Marx, and Joni untied *The Path of Righteousness* from the back of the full rigger. Marx studied the larger ship, *The Piercing Fin,* he read. Once it was free, they boarded and turned the *Path* around, steering it toward the left side of the cove that disappeared into the haze. Drifting along, the fog engulfed them. Joni let go of the helm; the ship steered itself—the sails drooped, lifeless.

"The gnome's system makes its way out here?" Marx asked.

Skye shook his head. "*She's* steering."

The seaweed scent struck. Large bunches hit the side of the boat as they sluggishly crept forward. The pirate's shouts and songs faded, replaced with *squish* and *drag*—the only sound. Even the gulls and wind avoided this place. A murky shadow swallowed them up as stalactites bit down. The jagged rocks were outlined by the dull light outside but soon, too, disappeared into the dark.

"Joni, you mind givin' us some light?" Skye asked.

The lantern only lit up the inside of the ship. Marx had to peer over the railing to see several white eyes glowing all around him.

"I see them too. No need to worry bout them. You heard of Torques?" Skye asked.

"Turtle people? I've heard of them. Never seen them before."

"They won't harm you," Skye assured.

Skye's assurance didn't diminish the uneasy feeling of the unseen creatures, hiding in the darkness, watching their every move. The entrance, a small hole of gray light at this range, told Marx they were far inside. The ship stopped.

Two large, blue, almond-shaped eyes loomed overhead. Several more sets of eyes cluttered around the ship. Skye grabbed a torch and pressed it against the lantern's glass—it caught. He walked to the bow. Torques: large turtle-like men, sharp beaks and large flat tails that wrapped around them. The beasts huddled close to a statue that rose over them all. The same statue that the large, blue eyes belonged to. They glinted in reflection to Skye's torch, revealing cut edges of sapphire stones. Marx's skepticism rose.

"Ah, my fellow blue-eyed wanderer. Glad to see you made it back," spoke a strange accent—a woman's voice that echoed throughout the cave.

"With your help I'm sure," Skye replied. "Although you never warned me about the storm."

"Did it not lead you right where you needed to be in order to acquire that new ship of yours?" the voice challenged. "Don't try to understand the ways of the gods. It will drive you mad. Who is your friend?"

"This is Marx."

"I sense something particularly different about him. A scent or stench. He's not an elf, is he?" Guagala asked.

"No, he's a human," Skye said.

"Hello, Guagala. Pleased to meet you." Marx shifted his gaze, trying to address the source of the voice.

"He acts like an elf."

"Do you know Nih?" Skye asked.

"This one follows him. That would explain it. Yes, of course I know him. I've known him since he first arrived on Iris with that sister of his. Poor girl, what happened to her."

"I've never heard of you until Skye brought you up. Are you a god as well? I thought Nih was the last one," Marx said.

"I don't care to credit myself with that title as he does. But I've been here long before those two showed up."

"In the days of Listar?" Marx asked.

The water's surface rippled in response, the boat rocked.

"Please excuse me. Best not to mention that name. He is gone, and for those closest to him, we say, good riddance. He broke our hearts with what he did," Guagala replied. "So, you follow a god who left the rest of the world to tend to the elves, his favorite. Interesting."

"I believe it is those who left him. Those who kill for profit, steal, and lie. The elves seem to be the only ones who understand this about the hearts of man, dwarf and o'ruk," Marx replied.

Guagala laughed, and with it, more rocking. "How the dull get duller. Believe what you want, human. I care very little about the subject.

"*Pirate*, you got something for my pets?"

"I do." Skye reached into his pockets and pulled out the round stones. "Magical heat rocks. I have four. Will that do?"

"You never cease to underpay me, pirate."

Skye threw the rocks at the feet of the torques. Their large tails dragged on the floor to gather the stones close.

"These are hard to come by, and although I have a few more, how can I visit you when I run out?" Skye said.

"You assume you have more reasons to see me. Now that I see my ship is back and intact, I can count that you did your part?" Guagala asked.

"I did. Those carved images were delivered." Skye answered. "I'd ask what that's all about but don't wanna get driven mad, trying to understand the gods and all."

"That's a wise pirate. Is there something else you need?" she asked.

"There are two more things. First, I plan to sail east, across the Unrested Sea. Is there anything I need to know about the waters there?" Skye asked.

"As there is always war on the minds of men, armies on Borenrang are building significantly. I would advise against a straight approach," Guagala answered.

"We aren't going to Borenrang, we're headed to Tinker's Ticker," Skye said.

"That would be safest. Most wouldn't dare land their ship on the gnome's homeland. Just keep your ship away from the trading routes and you'll fare just fine," Guagala returned. "And what is your second request?"

"My friend here needs a ship. This one will suit him just fine. Figure if you two could work out a deal," Skye asked.

"Well, human, is this true? Do you need a ship?" Guagala asked.

Marx paused before answering. "I don't have anything to give."

"I understand your dilemma. You don't want to betray your god. Don't worry. I won't ask you to bow down and worship me."

Heavy taps clicked around the hull, held firm, then dragged slowly. The lantern's small fire glinted off a row of bladed, finned-plates, each an arm's length. They stuck out of an enormous snake-like body. As they moved, the body wrapped around the boat completely. Marx heard Joni gulp and saw Skye's blue eyes widen. Finally, a serpent's head. Its long snout; pin-like teeth clamped against her closed mouth. The head rose well over the smaller statue that symbolized the goddess. Like mirrors, the thinly slitted eyes reflected the dancing flames coming from the boat.

"Go ahead and take it. A token of what a god *should* do for one of his followers."

Marx's heartbeat returned to normal as the ship made its way back to the lighter and louder part of the island. His suspicions were confirmed. Guagala was no god. He had heard tales of beings such as her but didn't think her kind still existed—until now. A group of beasts he thought were destroyed long ago; the Ancients. As Guagala confirmed, she was indeed here before Nih and Nil arrived to protect the world from Listar and his reign of horror. From what Marx could remember, the Ancients were Listar's most loyal servants. Taking the form of large animals, they were extremely powerful in magic. Not the typical, elemental magic but the ancient magic that flowed in many of those who lived thousands of years ago.

As his mind raced, he remembered the other religions around the world. Other regions and colonies worshipped all sorts of other false gods. He figured they were all intentionally and falsely conspired to trick the masses into falling in line. Or maybe that they were believed by those who needed to cling onto something that gave life a deeper meaning or a chance to reconcile the loss of their loved ones. Other than the basic ideas of each belief, Marx never gave it much thought. His first and only concern was for his dwarven brethren and their fairly new belief in the mountain god, Ulkralc. The influence he had and the statue they worshipped, a warthog. He'd never heard of a warthog Ancient, but he had heard of the sea serpent. Then, he remembered his dream. He now wished that he'd refused the ship. He wasn't sure how, but he felt her eyes on him.

"You okay? You sure don't seem all that happy to get a free boat. She made *me* sail halfway around the world for a delivery errand and told me to give it back when I was done with it."

Marx looked over the railing and into the water. He wasn't sure if Guagala could hear him but for whatever reason, figured she could.

"I get it. I'm still a bit spooked at seeing her face to face too. Joni boy here was about to swallow his own tongue." Skye slapped Joni on the back who admitted it with a smile.

"Yeah, I've never seen anything such as her. Intimidating to say the least," Marx said. "Time to get me back to Elet and the rest. It appears I have good news to tell her. As far as your debt with her is concerned, I'll make sure to let her know this was all your doing. Which is true."

The three made it back to the docks. Kork was there tinkering with an odd-looking box.

"What are you planning to do with those men down in the brig?" he said. "You plan on starving them to death?"

"Joni, you had a mind to use that Pip for something useful?" Skye threw Kork some rope to tie off the ship.

"I do," Joni replied.

"I'll be headed back now." Marx said. "Thank you for yet another tremendous tally on my adventure list. Care if I return to the other side of the island?"

"Not at all. What about your ship?" Skye asked.

Marx almost wanted to give it to Skye but wasn't sure how else to get Elet up north.

"Would you mind sailing it back to the gnome's side? When you have time, that is. No later than tomorrow?"

"That should be fine. Up at my hut, there's another fall line on the other side. That will take you to the central gnome hut. That's the quickest route. There, they will direct you where you need to go. Let your elf and gob friend know that we'll come collect them before dawn, if they're serious about joining. I will have my men sail your ship back to you then."

"You won't be joining them?" Marx asked.

"I will not."

"I believe we'll be departing tomorrow. Will I be seeing you again before then?" Marx said.

"I don't think so. I have plenty of plans to go over. I'd love to hear back from you if you're interested in joining me as well. I receive mail at Rimcaster Post. Guagala give you safe travels."

Marx reached out, gripped Skye's hand and pulled him close for a whispering word. "Be very wary of her. She is not who she says she is." Marx smiled as he let Skye go.

"Thank you. It was nice meeting you, Captain." Marx turned to Kork and Joni. "It was nice meeting all of you. I hope you accomplish making this world a better place."

Marx cut through the clouds as trees suddenly appeared ahead. Holding tight onto the leather straps, he braced, thinking he'd smack into the full branches below before he barely zipped past unscathed. His destination came into view. With such speed, he had to tuck and roll when he landed. Standing up, a gnome greeted him from behind a desk.

"Oh dear, looks like we measured wrongly. You should have landed much more gracefully. We apologize, Um Marx, is it?" the gnome said.

"Yes, and it's fine. I'm afraid any slower would minimize the thrill."

"You humans and your love of the thrill." The gnome chucked. "I was told you were coming. Come this way. We have your wife and children kept safely over here."

"Actually, they're just friends," Marx corrected.

"Are you the type of humans that don't get married?" the gnome asked as he scurried along.

"No, it's just that we're just friends," Marx returned.

"Oh, I see." He turned to eye Marx with concern.

Outside the bungalow, it branched out into three others. Choosing the path on their left, it ended with a small hut with nothing more than a large hole in its center.

"Here we are. This should take you to your friends, the dining area, or the showering room. I'm not entirely sure which, but I'm more certain than not, your friends." The gnome pondered, then nodded, pleased with his answer.

"Showering room?" Marx asked.

"No, no. Didn't you hear me? I said your friends. Hurry now, I have to get back." The gnome walked halfway before turning back. "Keep your arms to your sides. You'll need all that speed to get through without getting stuck."

Keeping that in mind, Marx examined the hole before entering. After setting both feet in, the slide pulled him through. The sun flickered through the holes as he descended quickly. Landing in some hallway, unsure where to go, he wandered in one direction until he saw a doorway, fabric draped over it.

"Hello?" he spoke before peeking inside, pulling his head back when he saw Elet's exposed skin. "I'm terribly sorry. I should have spoke louder."

Elet laughed. "It's okay. I wasn't fully undressed. Just a moment. There. Come on in."

Embarrassed, he almost wanted to ignore her invitation until the next awkward moment edged him inside. A white skirt came down to her knees; a matching tank top stopped just above her bellybutton. The white complemented her mocha skin. Her damp, dark red hair stuck against the back of her neck and shoulders. Where her yellow dress hid her athletic, petite features, this outfit showed. In all his travels, he'd truly never seen one such as she. He shifted his gaze aside; afraid he couldn't help staring.

"Did you guys have fun swimming?" he asked.

"We did. They are having quite the time here. Our little friends are interesting hosts to say the least. What about you? What was it Skye showed you? Pressing you to join his crew, I'm sure." Elet walked back into his view.

"That and to fulfill his promise to you. You know, he's not as bad as you thought. He got us that sailboat all to our own," Marx said.

"All to *our* own?" she asked with the same smile he looked forward to each day.

"Well, I…"

"I guess I *was* wrong about him. And what was your answer about joining him? Rifi and Kagu's chances just grew. Anything to get them off this side of the island. They're not loving the bombardment of the gnome's interrogation. It was as though they'd discovered an unnatural phenomenon."

"They *are* an unnatural phenomenon," Marx stated. "As for Skye, I haven't decided to join. He's an interesting man, that's for sure. We share similar interests, bettering the world that is. Although I can't admit my ambition is as strong."

"It sounds like maybe you should join. Following convictions births true merit. Don't shy away from them. The two of you could make quite the duo."

"I'm dedicated to helping you first. You and the siblings."

"The question then is, *why* is that?" she spoke before he could answer. "A question to ask yourself, in time.

"I see the way you treat them. Ethen, I've never seen a boy so driven. He's captivated in his training. And Kara, she told me about her past, and your influence; your plans to help her songs be heard."

"You have me at a disadvantage. I know very little about you. It's okay, I understand that sometimes it's best to have secrets. But can you tell me anything, like what's your life like back home?"

"I live a privileged life. Still, this little journey of ours has been more adventurous than all my days put together. It makes me wonder why I breathe. To be caged in luxury, or freed with nothing but the clothes I wear."

"Take it from someone who's traveled most of his life, *freed* is not the word I'd use."

"What would you call it then?"

"Unstable."

"Take it from someone who's spent her entire life being *stable,* a little instability isn't so bad." She smirked. "Looks like we're two sides of the same coin, Mr. Marx."

As their eyes refused to look away from one another, Marx's lips moved on their own. "So, do you live up by Lemwven?"

"I do. Well, that's the closest city."

"That's close to the elven woods. Do you live in some small town east of there?"

"No, west actually."

"West? How's that? I thought Lemwven is the limit, that no human can come any closer, and that the law is strictly enforced." Marx stopped himself. "Sorry, I don't mean to pry."

"It's okay. It's natural to wonder. And you're correct. No humans are allowed to visit where I live. I am an exception."

Marx ignored the urge to ask further.

Elet edged closer, no more than an inch but more than enough to double Marx's heart rate. He wanted to move closer. Her eyes begged him to. In combat, he never hesitated to react swiftly, but here he was caught. In between passion and unfamiliar territory, something much stronger and stranger than an urge.

"Did you see those twirly doohickies?" Kara came in like a forging hammer, breaking the spell; Ethen behind her. "Hey Marx. When'd you get back? Oh… sorry was I interrupting something?"

Not catching the mood, Ethen continued, "Marx, I'm ready to train if you are."

"No, Ethen. They're um…" Kara mildly coughed while tilting her eyes in Marx and Elet's direction.

"Oh…" Ethen paused.

"No, it's okay. We were just talking," Marx fumbled.

"Um right," Kara replied, rolling her eyes.

"Kara, we *were* just talking. Please don't be rude," Elet said firmly. "You're making Marx blush."

The siblings laughed, and Elet joined. Finally, Marx cracked a smile before walking past Ethen with a shoulder tap. "Come now, we're wasting useful daylight. Ladies, if you'll excuse us."

Before Ethen followed Marx, he ran to grab his sword and shield, they were in another room around the hall. Asking around, they were advised the best place to train was surely the overview, a large deck overlooking the beach below.

"Do you remember the stances I taught you?" Marx asked.

"Yes."

"Which do you like most?"

"I'm not sure."

"Teaching you those stances lays out some options. Your job is to find one that feels right." Marx grabbed the hilt of his sword.

"There are many more than what I taught. With the ones you know are the standards. Mine is this." Marx stood straight before leaning back slightly. He held his tip straight to the ground. "This is the one I showed you, *the current.*"

"It doesn't look like the current," Ethen pointed out.

"That's because it's a variant. It had taken me a bit of knowing myself; my strengths and weaknesses, before I knew this to be my most effective stance. So, if you don't yet know yours, that's for the best. Just be on the lookout for it.

"While you're on the lookout, here is the next key to understanding the best attack, the best defense. You can only defend an oncoming attack." Marx raised his weapon and brought it down. Ethen knew to step aside before the block. "Good," Marx said and shoved the end of his scabbard into Ethen's gut. Ethen's next breath was taken from him.

"I have taught you the basics of defending an oncoming attack. However, your eyes are on the weapon itself." Marx shook his head. "Understanding your enemy's anatomy will grant you the ability to determine his end result. Instead of focusing on the weapon, focus on his center."

Marx swung his weapon in nine different, distinct attacks.

"Do you see? Your eyes followed my movement much faster than my outward blade. My center holds together my arms, my arms, hands, my hands, the blade's attack. So, my center displays my very intention so you can read what attacks I have in mind. Understand?"

"I think so," Ethen said.

"Good, here." Marx swung swiftly; Ethen blocked the attack.

Three more attacks and a grin formed on Ethen's face.

"Assuming both opponents have equal stamina, the attacker will use more energy. Sometimes, it's best to block your opponent and let him weary himself out before you switch to the offensive. One way to cause this is to taunt your opponent. That I'll teach you another day but know there are many ways to taunt, not all are mocking. Sometimes, simply edging closer or giving the appearance that *you* are the attacker can spur an attack."

Marx struck five more times, all of which Ethen saw coming and defended.

"Very good. Do you remember *The Storm* stance?" Ethen nodded. "Good. Show me."

Marx searched for balance in both Ethen's reaction, which Marx called the *spring*, and his appearance called the *wall*.

"The Storm's not for you. What do you think?"

"It feels weird."

"Then we move on."

A couple hours passed as Marx searched for a stance that fit, finding none.

"Don't feel bad. This can be beneficial. Clearing up the standards means you're likely to find a stance that will throw most opponents off." Movement on the sunset's reflection drew Marx's attention. The Path of Righteousness arrived on shore. Marx slid his weapon into its scabbard, letting Ethen know they were done for the day.

"Good job. I have to go get our new boat."

"*Our* boat?" Ethen asked.

"Come on, let's go say our goodbyes to Rifi and Kagu. I think they've decided to join Skye."

Finding their way down to the beach, Marx met with the pirates dropping off his ship; Kara joined. The pirates untied a rowboat from the Path while Rifi and Kagu stood next to it, ready to board

"Well, it was nice knowing you all," Rifi said.

"Now forever gone?" Kagu asked.

"No, no. Not forever gone. Some other time gone," Rifi said before looking back at the siblings. "Right?"

"I hope so," Kara said, seeing Kagu's expression change. "I mean, um yes. Some other time gone."

Rifi extended his hand, Kara took it and pulled him in for a hug. More hugs and handshakes were exchanged before they boarded and rowed off. Marx and the siblings watched until the rowboat disappeared behind the bend of the island. Not long after, the sun joined, disappearing behind the horizon.

Marx, Elet and the siblings gathered in the dining area; a large back deck facing away from the beach. The tropical forest beneath them was put on display by several lit torches. Dozens of other gnomes and few humans sat at the same dinner table that curved around like an uncoiled snake. Dinner was served, and most was eaten. Some dishes were enjoyed while others were politely spit out into table cloths and some too strange to gauge.

"Food is something we're afraid we'll never master. Far too many ingredients and subjective tastebud receptors," Bell said. "Doesn't mean we don't have fun exploring what works and what doesn't." She reached for the plates that all had the same uneaten food still on them. "We'll mark this down as *what doesn't.*"

After dinner, Marx was given directions to his room where he wanted to run to. After every gnome was told that Elet was in fact *not* his wife, comments came and never seemed to cease. Comments such as:

"But they make such a cute couple."

"Isn't *that* curious?"

"Wonder if everything works down there."

"I've heard procreation isn't for everyone."

When the comments *did* stop, they were excused and led toward their side of the island. With the amount of embarrassment, Marx wanted nothing more than to escort Elet to her room and walk away. Kara didn't help by winking as she hurried Ethen along and ahead into their own room, leaving Marx and Elet alone.

"I guess *subtlety* is not the gnome's strong suit." Elet chuckled.

"No, I suppose it's not."

"Thank you for the company, and the laughs."

"Happy to oblige. Now if you'll excuse me, with the amount of embarrassment, I think I'm going to jump off the island's peak," Marx said.

"It was nice knowing you. You'll surely be missed."

"Good night, Elet," Marx said after the playful smiles faded.

"Night, Marx." As he walked halfway down the hall, she added. "Although I yearn to be back home, I also dread that day, the thought that it could be our last together."

"Me too." Marx waved and forced his legs to keep walking.

As he continued, a lit torch caught his eye down a side hallway. There a human stood alone, it was Phin. Walking behind him, Marx stepped loudly to announce his arrival.

"Good evening," Marx said.

"To you as well," Phin returned, an artificial smile hanging.

"Everything okay?" Marx asked.

"As it can be."

"Did you have a chance to cast your spell?"

"Um, unfortunately, no. I'm afraid the spell is too complex. Every syllable is uniquely pronounced, and each one needs to be precise. If they aren't, the entire spell, and the endless study, is wasted. We live in a time when getting advice from the ones who mastered the art is simply lost. At times, I wonder if I should give this life up. I'm not too old to spend the rest of my days relaxing on one of these islands."

"Doesn't sound too bad to me," Marx said.

"Doesn't it though? When you love something, it's worth the chase. Whether you receive it in the end or not. What is love if not that?"

"Are you saying that the chase alone tells you what you love?"

"I think that's part of it. I've seen many chase the wrong things all their lives, only to find bitterness as their reward. Loving the chase is a good way to find that fulfillment."

"I'm not sure I've chased fulfillment in all my life. I suppose I've only hoped contentment would fall flat on my lap." Marx watched the orange light flicker off the large leaves below.

"You guys leaving tomorrow?" Phin asked.

"We are. Long few days ahead. I should be going to bed now. It was nice meeting you. You've given me a lot to think about. Good luck with that spell and be careful in this world of ours." Marx bowed, walked to his room, got on his knees, prayed, and fell asleep.

Chapter Ten

Unlikely Recruit

Rifi and Kagu were brought to Skye's side of the island. A massive firepit lit up much of the cove, with a couple hundred men huddled around it. The pirates' hollering gave away their drunkenness, although all were not drunk. Captain Skye Larker awaited the rowboat.

"The crux to our entire operation," Skye teased as the boat came into sight. "Welcome. We're glad to have ya."

"I can see you guys know how to have fun. Reminds me of the Barrel. So, when does this whole initiation start?" Rifi asked.

"It's nothing fancy; just an oath, and an oath is only as good as one's desire to fulfill it. All I ask..." Skye extended his hand as the boat touched the dock, "...is you look around and ask yourself if this is the family you want to embrace. We share the spoils and stand up for each other. And that means death if need be. However, I've yet to lead one to any sort of sacrifice just as I never led my men to kill the defenseless. Our conquest is ultimately peace, but that means a few men who hold the world's power must step aside or die in the process.

"The world is a deceitful place, and the governments who run it have led the people astray with promises of prizes, such as prosperity and peace. They lie secretly, leading good men to war, ordering husbands and fathers to sell their souls, killing the innocent. You think they'd give a copper coin to their widows and orphans? Think twice on that.

"We look to change the world and now you have a glimpse of our aim. Do you share this aim?" Skye asked.

"Yeesh, that's pretty deep." Rifi scratched his head. "I get your point. Part of the reason I steal is to take back from those who guard their riches, leaving nothing for the rest of us. Yeah, alright, I'm game. Um, Kagu?" Rifi looked over to his goblin friend who was staring off toward the fire, not paying attention in the least. "Kagu?!"

"Big fire flame."

"That's probably the best of a *yes* you can hope for," Rifi said.

"Actually, I'm not accepting at this time. This should not be a rash decision." Skye turned toward the fire. "First, go, enjoy yourself. You already know much of the crew.

Ask questions, get answers. What *do* you want to accomplish with your one life? Once you have the answers you seek, come find me." Skye tipped his hat and walked away.

"Okay, thanks, Captain," Rifi replied as he turned to Kagu. "Come on bud. Let's go check out that fire. No matter how pretty it is, don't jump in."

"You mess fun time," Kagu replied, disappointed.

"I just want you to live to see the age of twelve is all."

The Laneloon captives were tied up, both hands and feet, as they shuffled past the fire and led into a large, crashed ship at the back side of the cove. When they arrived, they found Joni waiting. The pirates delivered the men, turned back, and joined the others around the fire. Joni soaked himself in the silence, as the men were forced to relive the way they treated him, some worse than others; no one worse than Pip. The way Pip blubbered and cowardly denied the chance to fight their traitor and free the Watchmen, the men spat and insulted him way past the way he'd ever treated Joni.

"What do you plan to do with us traitor?" one asked.

Joni just smiled back, watching the men as if enjoying a climactic scene in a play. Others joined in on the questioning, some pleading, some angry and some just trying to get a response. Still, nothing. Soon after they were worn down to silence, Skye entered.

"You been keepin them in line Joni boy?" Skye asked.

"In my own way."

Skye hardened as he strolled past the band of prisoners. He took his time, locking eyes with each one. His piercing blue eyes, peered deep within each, searching for true desires. His eyes landed on the last man, Pip. Although Pip's desires were displayed before, Skye stared into his eyes the longest.

"These last days haven't been kind, aye?" Skye spoke firm. "Not due to the way these men have treated you but the understanding of what you know about yourself. A coward's fiercest enemy is himself. The thing is, they usually don't know this truth, but you do."

Pip tried to avoid Skye's eyes but couldn't look away. Just as he tried to avoid this inescapable truth. There was no more hiding. It was time to accept it.

"Please, take my life. I can't escape who I am," Pip said, his despaired eyes pleading.

"Joni, can you take it from here? I need to know if these men's lives are worth a piss. As for Pip here…" Skye unsheathed his sword and struck. Pip winced.

The rope that bound Pip's feet was sliced through. The next were those that bound his hands.

"I would like to have a word with this one here," Skye said.

"Aye Sir," Joni said, eyeing the men.

"Follow me." Skye turned his back and walked out. Struck, Pip's emotions came crashing, colliding with an uncertainty to follow. Giving his old Watchmen and Joni a glance, following Skye was an extended hand he was willing to take.

When Pip stepped out, Skye's back was still turned to him. The sign of trust dispelled any thoughts of escape or attack. More so, it was the truth Skye pointed out. A truth that he could no longer run from.

"Follow me," Skye said gently as he walked into the shadows of the rocks overhead.

Joni stood and looked around; he was alone. Another thought of escape fled with curiosity. Away from all the firelight, the rocks were lit by the Lux instead. The shine, the outline of Skye's leather coat, drew him closer. He watched the captain sitting, overlooking the giant fire, his men, and the sea. He lit his pipe. The orange ember glowed, igniting his face and his clumps of beaded hair that framed it.

"Do you know why I do what I do?" Skye asked.

The thought never entered Pip's mind until now.

"Because of my immoral desire to live out a life of wickedness?" Skye spoke Pip's thoughts. "What would you consider moral? Or wickedness for that matter?"

A moment passed. "Wickedness is the absence of morality," Pip said.

"That's obvious. So, what is morality to you?"

"Peace. That ship you stole protected Laneloon Harbor and with it gone, they are more vulnerable."

"That ain't a bad answer. But do you not think they're overly protected? That the southern neighbors wouldn't protect them or that a formidable enemy would travel the strait unnoticed? Not only that but Laneloon is a benefit to the world, even to enemies of Tanenfalle. All to say, it isn't the most strategic place to attack.

"Paranoia gets the better of man. Fear fuels war, not a search for peace. To find peace, we need to find those who create the fear. Those who *drive* it, find profit from it. And whether you know it or not, they are the very ones paying your salary. You showed your cards already, fear has driven you to the point of enslavement, that much is apparent not just to me, but to those men who once called you Sir.

"I have a different answer. Morality isn't based on the principles of our nature, wickedness is. Morality is that something inside us that tugs when we stray away from that nature, while wickedness provides pleasure when we align ourselves with it. Morality, without contest, is the harder journey up the hill when all we want to do is slide to the bottom. I think that's what you've been experiencing the last few days, the bottom.

"But what do I know? Most people think their side is the moral one. Even if they intentionally plant weeds in the hearts of the very ones they swear to protect and die for. You and your late captain have planted weeds in those men back there. I seek to rip them out from the ground and re-soil them. What do you seek, truly? Aside from the sharp end of my blade? What did you want before you became a lapdog of those govies?"

A pause lasted before an answer came. "Believe it or not, I wanted nothing more than to sail. At a young age I learned everything I could about ships. That got me in with the fleet where I saw an opportunity to sail and to seek peace."

"Were you a stiff necked browbeat back then?" Skye asked.

"No, I wasn't." An unexpected chuckle escaped him. "*I* was the one who got the raw end of the beating stick. Fact is, I've never liked fighting."

"Were you given that beating stick at home or in the fleet?"

"I suppose both. I never found the peace I wanted."

"So, you resented the world?"

The silence was enough to answer.

"There!" Skye shouted. "Right there. You had a chance to push toward the top of that hill, to show yourself and everyone how badly you really wanted that peace. Rather, you slid back down with the rest of the world.

"It's okay lad. It's what separates the few from the masses. Part of the problem is those who want peace don't exactly know how to achieve it. Also, they aren't willing to do what it takes, afraid of what the world will do to them if they continue. And those who *are* willing to do something, they die in battles that are in a direct contradiction with what peace obviously is. Ironic to say the least. I have seen this for a while now and so although, I admit I don't yet know how to go about bringing peace, I assure you, I, too, desire the same thing."

"What now? Are you offering me a life of piracy? To betray the oath, I have sworn?"

"Nah. With your display back on the ship, I couldn't afford to. I'd lose trust. I wonder though, if you'd be willing to work together to bring that peace, we both want. You'd have to forgive the ship I stole and in return, I'd return you to Laneloon. I hope then we can establish some trust. Just know, I already expect you to betray me, but you will have a chance to prove me wrong. At that time, you will have gained a friend."

"What is it exactly you want?" Pip asked.

Skye reached into his pocket and withdrew a leatherbound flask, took a drink, and passed it to Pip. "I'm glad you asked."

Kagu plunged his hand into the fire. Rifi kept breaking his conversation to yank his friend back, stopping him from burning his flesh beyond repair.

"Doesn't the little guy feel that heat?" Nathan asked, a pirate Rifi had met aboard the Fin.

"Nope. Didn't you know? Goblins don't feel pain." Rifi grabbed Kagu by the wrist and quickly shackled him to himself. "I didn't want to do that, but you gave me no choice."

Kagu puffed a long sigh.

"I did hear that, but I guess I didn't believe it. And they don't fear nothin either?"

"Nope. Sure, they're small but an army of em are a nasty sight. Reason o'ruks use them when they can. Kagu here is different though because most usually lack any kind of empathy. Kagu is as sweet as a firefly. Kagu stop it!"

Kagu was caught gnawing on his hand in hopes to free himself.

"Here, I'll let you go if you promise me to leave that fire alone," Rifi said sternly.

"Fine, no fire feel," Kagu promised.

"So, I thought pirates were all about killing and pillaging and stuff," Rifi said as he unlocked Kagu.

"Not us. Although there are those sorts, fer sure. Some here used to be those sorts. You met Joni, he was one born under that cruel lifestyle. Skye gave him, gave all us a better proposition."

"What's that?"

"Fer starters, the pay's better. And most people, aside from the worst, don't like killin' for no good reason. Skye finds the good in people, especially us seacrooks."

"You admire him."

"Most of us misfits live the way we do because we stray from a purpose. He gives us one. Plus, he ain't no pusher. He helps out like the rest. Maybe even more. He is the only captain I've ever known or heard worth serving under."

"How are you going to accomplish this world-peace mission?"

"That is the question, my little elf friend. It ain't gonna be easy. You from the Thieves' Trade, right?" Nathan said.

"We don't like titles but yeah."

"They figured out something worthwhile, that underground networking of theirs. We have something similar. On land, we have spies seeking those taken advantage by their government. Most of em are farmers or workers, some small market owners. We pay them for the word around, we gain their trust, then we take from those who take from them. Like that ship we stole. Those Laneloon folk, as far as their govies know, are none the wiser, so they have nothing to lose. This applies to all we deal with. We do a fair job making it appear that *they* gotten ripped off, when they barter those goods with our coin. It's a win win for us and the common folk and a lose for the power hungry."

"Is that it? We rip them off to death," Rifi asked.

"No, not entirely. Skye's brewing somethin. There's much to gain by keeping silent while exposing the govies dark intent. To secretly spread the message like you thieves do about a big score. Patience is the general plan; to crumble corrupt empires from the inside out by turning their own people against them. Other than that, I have no idea how that's to come about. But Skye reminds us that one of the things he ponders on nonstop, that each one of us has a big role. He dismisses the idea that all it takes is one willing; rather, it will take each of us, dependent on the other. Then, nothing can stop us."

"I've never thought that *I* could be some hero," Rifi said.

"That's the thing the captain sees in each of us. And not just fluffy talk but practical ways, to do the unthinkable. You were a witness to how easily he took over that ship. All premeditative, trust, and faith in each of those involved. Can you see your thieves group do anything of the sort?"

"Not really. When they work together, they're already thinking about how they'll take the rest for themselves," Rifi said.

"So, ask yourself what's better ultimately—to get by or peace? The vision the captain shows us is that we can achieve both. There is enough wealth in the world for everyone. It's those greedy hoarders that want it all for themselves. We look to strip them dry, take our cut and disperse the rest to those under em."

"How do you not know that greed won't corrupt you guys?"

"That's another thing, the captain is good at showing us. Contentment is worth more than all the money in the world. Sometimes it's the blood and tears that shows us that it's not worth all those greedy thoughts. Peace *and* to get by is our goal. We just want the rest of the world who want the same thing to be a part of it."

"I never heard nobility make so much sense," Rifi replied.

"Oi, Panfry?" the pirate yelled across the fire. "Where in the seas have you been?" Nathan turned to Rifi. "Excuse me, I have to go talk to this sorry excuse of a sailor."

"By all means. Thanks for the talk," Rifi said with a wave.

Rifi stared into the fire a few long moments, dwelling on his conversation with the pirate. At the age of a hundred and eight, he'd outlived one generation of humans. Part of the reason he fled his homeland, he enjoyed humans, their fun and strange logic. His fellow elves were always so spiritual, thinking nothing but the life after this one. Sure, the humans *were* wicked at times, seeming to desire nothing but their own destruction.

However, why Rifi decided to live among them at the young-elf age of fifty-two, he felt a tug to help them.

Looking back, he realized his elf family was right in many ways—that humans corrupt. The ones he chose to dwell with seemed beyond help and admittedly *had* corrupted Rifi in more ways than one. He feared that perhaps he was wicked. He eventually understood humans have a twisted way to achieve their version of what *they thought* was right. The thought came to him here and there: that maybe he should go home, ask for forgiveness, get cleansed, and never return to the rest of the world. There was a part of him that missed his friends and family dearly.

His other part wanted to live out the tug he received decades ago. Kagu, believed by his elves to be a spawn of the shadows, was a recent sign that maybe his kin were wrong. Kagu in many ways was the evidence he needed to stay outside of the elven sanctuary. He saw good in his green friend. He wanted to protect Kagu and live that out to see where it led. If it led to the darkness his elves were sure it would lead, he would at least get his answer and go back home.

What if Skye was an answer to the tug he'd been waiting for all this time. An actual way to fix the brokenness of the humans. A sign that they do want peace but are too rambunctious, dimwitted, and too short of lives to accomplish it. Maybe Skye, as jokingly as he was, did need Rifi and Kagu more than he knew. That the two natural enemies could show the world how peace is possible in a most drastic way.

Laughter roared from a group of pirates that surrounded Kagu. A bit of joy was found in the goblin's beady eyes and a smile that Rifi never got sick of seeing; it cracked open to join the laughter. Rifi walked among the men, "Any of you see the Captain? Need to tell him something."

Chapter Eleven

Speechless Serpent

Trashing. Disaster. A splitting squawk freed Marx from his paralyzed state. Shooting up, the heavy sleep hung in his head. As he looked back down at his pillow, every inch of his desire wanted to lay back down. Another squawk, suggested otherwise. He shook his head, fighting the grog before standing up. Images of his dream were blurred and blotched. Three green and red parrots faced him from outside his window. With a few reps of in-place sprints and climber planks, his blood circulated, and the heavy sleep was forgotten as was his dream. Satisfied that he was up, the parrots flapped in unison with their departure.

It was first hour. Peering out the window, the little busy-bodied gnomes filled the tiny homes and bridges dispersed throughout the branches. Down the hallway, he peeked into the siblings' room. Kara still lay asleep while Ethen faced the window with the beach below, cleaning his sword. Marx didn't interrupt him. As he watched, his own early years admiring his first blade came back like a familiar smell—how he would clean it the same way and how determined he was to use it well. Then his first kill interrupted, tarnishing the early memory. All his training never prepared him for the effect that it left behind. Perhaps Ethen's next lesson would focus on that alone.

"Morning, Ethen. She clean?" Marx whispered as he stepped in.

"Yeah," Ethen replied.

"What is it that drives you to know the sword?"

"The strength it comes with." The answer was quick.

"You know, strength is a tool. How do you know you'll be on the right side of the steel?"

"What do you mean? I won't hurt people if that's what you mean."

"You won't hurt people? Not even those who deserve it?"

"I will *those* people. I mean I won't hurt innocent people."

"Most think that they're innocent and all have a reason why they are the way they are," Marx said. "I'm not excusing evil because it does exist. I'm pointing out that some do what they do because evil may have visited *them* at one point or another. The true and best weapon is the way of the heart. You change that, and most evil of men can turn from the dark path they travel. You will not only win your own life and theirs, but any they might harm."

"What if I can't change his heart?" Ethen asked.

"Unfortunately, you can't always and so you do what you must. However, search for that opening, the opening of the heart. If it's available, it should be the primary attack." Marx turned as Kara stirred in bed. "I'll let you two get ready. We have a lot of traveling ahead of us."

Marx exited the room and walked up to Elet's. He made sure to shout her name this time. No answer. Peering in, he found the room empty. He walked to the same deck he trained Ethen. There, he could see the beach and The Path of Righteousness safe. He wondered if the sky would be clear on their travels.

His thoughts went to Laneloon and whether or not they'd have trouble passing by. There was no evidence that he or the others were involved in the heist. Still, he figured he'd keep a distance from the harbor before entering the strait. He was certain the harbor's concern would be on The Piercing Fin alone. Or so he hoped.

Elet came into view a few floors down. She was ready to leave it seemed, carrying her own bags. Marx told the siblings to grab their things and meet him below in the dining area. As he made his way down, Elet sat alone with her bow and a quiver strapped to her backside. Her outfit was leather—light beige. It was a bit loose for comfort and clean. It covered most of her center while allowing the rest of her skin to breathe. Marx realized she never found a way to be any less beautiful. She sat looking away from him, nibbling on an assortment of cut-up pieces of tropical fruits the island provided.

"I think I'll have what you're having. I can't trust the gnome's recipes," Marx said as he came from behind. "Morning Elet."

"Morning, Marx. Sleep well?" She turned to lock eyes, providing that smile.

"I slept pretty heavy. It was hard to get up. You ready to travel? What am I saying? You've been ready to travel for days already. I'm happy to get a move on. Kara and Ethen should be coming down any minute. I saw some of your bird friends in my room."

"Bird friends?"

"Yeah, the same kind I saw you talking to before we set sail," Marx said. "Any chance you could ask them for a weather report?"

"I'll have that," Kara interrupted, pointing at the Elet's bowl of fruit.

"Me too," Ethen seconded.

"We might need to get all that we can from our friends here. We have a long way to sail, just shy of a week." Marx noticed Bell walking up.

"Aww, that's a sorry sight. Look at those bags. You ready to leave us so soon? You just got here," Bell said.

"I'm afraid so," Marx said.

"It was a pleasure having you, just a pleasure. I hope to see you back. If you can get to Rimcaster, you can get here. Just head southwest until you hit the overcast and smell of seaweed," Bell said.

"Thank you very much for everything, Bell," Elet said.

"Yes, your hospitality is unmatched," Marx added, kneeling to bow to her level.

"Aren't you quite the charmer? You know if you two never get married, you can always come back and marry me," Bell teased. "Now go on. Best to sail early and you've already wasted plenty of time on me. Here, before you go, let me grab you some snacks." Bell brought two large sacks full of food, some questionable, unless they found themselves stranded.

Bell led them down to the beach.

"Do come back now," Bell said, her large eyes shining. "Come in, let's get those hugs and these goodbyes over with."

One by one, they boarded in the Path. They looked back at the strange island that whistled, steamed, and banged with all sorts of moving contraptions. Whatever held the ship from under let go as a gust of wind got caught in the sails pushing them out to sea. The island shrank as they sailed away. The ship stopped; its sails still full.

"What now?" Kara said, looking overboard.

"We're probably just caught on some hooks," Marx said, peering over the bow.

Several large tails swayed in the water. Torques held the ship in place. The flat tails pushed back, keeping the ship from moving. Marx pulled his sword free.

"Let us go," he yelled at the only torque who surfaced.

Wide face, sharp beak, black eyes stared back, unmoved, and unthreatened.

"Give them the pendant and you and your human friends can go free," Guagala's voice was heard from the water itself, from all around.

Marx cursed. The boat shook violently, rocking to the point that it nearly tipped over. Marx quickly reached down the front part of his pants.

"Marx! What in the world are you doing?" Elet shouted.

He gripped. Time slowed. Marx then grabbed Ethen by the collar, using the appropriate speed he launched him. Next, Kara and finally Elet. Before throwing her, time returned. "Get the kids to land," he stressed. Time slowed once again, and Elet was flung.

Marx returned to the bow and looked over, the torques were practically still, caught in time. A chant rang. Something he'd heard only once before. A doubled voice, impossible to mimic, echoed as it cut through the air, catching up to Marx sped-up self. This ancient spell was one of its kind, one he'd heard before. He tensed up.

A line of water spewed upward and froze, suspended in the air as it came at him. He readied his blade. The water stopped before the boat. A shadow blocked the sun. Guagala's tail flew over the main deck. The girth equaled the ship itself, dwarfing Marx. She quickly coiled around the Path. Marx sprinted, pulled back, then forward trying to plunge his blade into her body. The diamond shaped scales were too large and thick. Marx aimed to pry and dig his blade under any one scale, but each covered another and moved far too fast. He knew with his speed another attack would damage his weapon. The end of the tail came again wrapping the ship a second time and once more.

Her tail tightened as the boat tensed. Floorboards shifted and buckled. Marx knelt and jumped, returning time to normal to fly up. The Path of Righteousness suddenly collapsed within itself and brought into the sea in an instant. Slowing time back down, Marx brushed his feet against the water's surface. Step by step, he propelled himself forward, jetting for land.

With a glance back, another line of water shot up, moving at him. Doubt drowned his chances; she gained on him too quickly. Her enormous body burst from the sea, gaping her mouth, too large to escape; dozens of fishbone teeth sprawled at him.

Curl up, a voice spoke. Confused, Marx wasn't sure how that would help

Now, the voice said with authority. He knew to trust it.

Marx curled up as Guagala came down, swallowing him whole. He nearly missed her narrow teeth, each begging to pierce him through. Darkness engulfed him. Guagala's slimy tongue, the size as Marx, twisted around, pushing him into the side of her mouth where her teeth waited to shred him apart.

Strike down, hold. He obeyed; the blade only dug so far. *Press your foot down; push deeper.* Marx did. Her head shook violently in response. *Don't let go. Keep digging. There. You almost have it.*

Sunlight burst. The giant mouth flung open, spitting Marx and the severed tongue out. Guagala froze, left behind in normal time. Marx used his reserved energy to run on the water, back to land. Several torques were on shore, trapped, tangled in what must have been the rope system the gnomes had made. He saw Elet, Kara and Ethen safe. He came to them, time returned.

"Marx!" Elet shouted, startled at the sudden appearance. "I thought you were…"

"How did you..." Ethen yelled.

"You okay?" Kara asked.

"I'm fine, I'm fine." Marx looked up. "Someone is watching over me."

"Shoo, shoo." Bell came running up, yelling at the stuck torques. Turning back to her fellow gnomes she yelled. "Command seven F four. That's seven F four."

Gnomes shouted, repeating the order until it reached the center of the island. An object flew from a giant slingshot, hung out from one of the buildings. Whatever it was, it landed in the water surrounding the torques. Bubbles fizzled. The torque squirmed and finally detached themselves from the ropes and fled.

"What was that?" Marx asked.

"Don't really have a name for it. A combination of chemicals. It won't kill em but they'll be irritated for days," Bell answered. "I always warn Skye not to get too friendly to that sea witch. Something about her gives me the graspy peekies. Say, how'd you throw these fellers so far? I just *got* to study whatever that is."

"Sorry, Bell. I cannot say." Marx slid his blade into his scabbard. "As for Guagala, I cut out her tongue. She convinced Skye that she is some god, I just proved she's a liar. Without her tongue to chant, her power is much less."

"Much less a liar now too," Bell chuckled.

"Why did she come after you?" Elet asked.

"I'm sorry, I can't say, to save you from trouble, I promise." Marx turned to Kara. "Rifi, how well do you know him? How well do you trust him?"

"Well, he's a thief but as far as thieves go, he's okay," Kara answered.

"He was the only one who knew," Marx said. "It seems he's betrayed us."

"I don't think he'd know we'd all be eaten up," Kara said.

"I don't think you're wrong. But if all those pirates know, we're in trouble. I have to go talk to Skye *and* Rifi, to set things straight. Bell is there another way to Skye's side of the island. One that avoids the sea?" Marx asked.

"Here, come now follow me," Bell said. "You know, I wished you'd be back early, ha. Wasn't expecting *this* early and under such yucky circumstances."

"*Now* how are we going to go north?" Elet asked.

"Another reason to talk to Skye," Marx said.

The group followed Bell into an underground room. Shelves full of books and tables full of maps and math scribbles were spread unevenly across the room. A few gnomes were found, each assigned a table as they sat quietly, absorbed in study.

"Shh, this is our *inventing-plan* room," Bell whispered. "We sometimes have to get away from the whistling teapot outside. Ah, Phin, no surprise to find you here. He also enjoys the quiet."

Phin sat at the room's end. Open books and papers placed in front of him, filled with strange letters and sigils. Phin turned.

"Marx?" Phin said, surprised. "I thought you had left. What has kept you?"

"Guagala," Bell answered for him.

"What happened?" Phin asked.

"She attacked my ship. Destroyed it in the process," Marx answered.

"He is about to go see Skye now," Bell informed.

"I wonder why she attacked you. I have always felt something strange about her," Phin said.

"*Me* too!" Bell agreed.

"Shh…" a nearby gnome hushed.

"Bell, I can escort them to the other side of the island. I was planning on making that trip today anyways. I truly need a break from my studies." Phin stood up, marking one book with the pages lying in front of it. He layered them each carefully, in a particular way and in a particular order. Carefully folding the pages that stuck out he bent them over other pages, closed the book and slid it into his bookbag, strapped over his shoulder. "I can take it from here Bell."

"You are always such a doll, Phin. Oh, dolphin! Ha, that nickname's not going away anytime soon," Bell chuckled and bid them all, again, farewell.

"Do you know why Guagala attacked you?" Phin asked as he led the way into a dark tunnel.

"That's what I plan to figure out," Marx said.

"You don't think Skye had anything to do with the attack, do you?"

"I don't know. What I *do* know is he follows her, and he introduced me just yesterday,"

"I have a hard time believing he knew what she did. But you're right. Best way to know is go ask the man himself."

They emerged from a wide hole, up into a tropical scenery. A few clear, turquoise waterfalls fell separately into a single shallow pool. A random assortment of brightly colored flowers stood out in contrast to the bright and dark green leaves.

"How far we going?" Kara asked.

"It's about a two-mile hike around the peak," Phin answered. "Shouldn't take much more than an hour.

A spark split through the crack of Skye's eyelids. His fuzzed comprehension only reminded him of the night before; discussions with his men and potential recruits. Disappointment yet admiration for those who rejected his leadership and therefore death. After, late hours added late drinks; the songs still rang as the sun persistently pestered him. His hair held an irregular amount of sand, dug deep, scratching his cranium. A small chug of brandy pushed back the throb. Standing up he let the air rise, taking a moment to fill his head and settle back.

Climbing down into his small shack, he pet his feline friend who responded with a loud cry and a humming purr.

"Smidgens, dear boy, you really have to get some new friends." Skye scratched behind Smidgens' ear who pushed back until he fell over. "Since you have no sense to listen, hold down the fort until I get back, will ya?"

Smidgens meowed in disapproval.

"I know, I just got back but I have duties." Skye walked out and added. "While don't you make yourself useful and clean up while I'm gone."

Skye slid down the rope-line toward the shore. The number of bodies scattered around looked as though a battle had occurred.

"Look at you good-for-nothins," Skye commented cheekily as he stepped over those in his way.

He arrived in one of the smaller crashed ships, the one belonging to Kork. The gnome was found at his table, at work. Bananas, oranges, pineapples, tomatoes and carrots had been tossed on the floor.

"Any new gain?" Skye asked.

"Indeed, I have. You can say it has been *fruit*ful.*"

"Please, spare me. My head hurts too much for lame jests."

"I have found what fruits and vegetables are surely a weak source. Citrus *does* conduct but not as well as the faithful potato. Still, I wonder if I could extract the citrus from the orange and lime to create a more effective current somehow. We have plans back home, but it shouldn't take me long before I beat ol' Phin at our friendly race." (Wizards and gnomes are known to compete; science to magic) Kork looked away from his project to face Skye with thick spectacles that enhanced his already large eyes. "What of you? Any new gain from those you captured?"

"Aye, some have decided to join while others, I'm sad to say, will be answering to Guagala."

"That's a nasty business you run." Kork looked back at his work.

"I can only hope it's worth it," Skye said.

"And we gnomes are the ones accused of wasting time on meaningless projects. At least ours doesn't involve deaths. Well, not on purpose."

"I have to believe it's not meaningless. At least the deaths are few compared to government machines that turn them out by the thousands."

Kork mumbled to himself, some scientific mumbo jumbo.

"Anyways, you know what's about to happen. Just wanted to steer clear, in case," Skye warned.

"Yeah, yeah." Kork shoed him away.

Skye entered another crashed ship near, where the prisoners were held. He collected a few bystanding crewmen on his way. Shackled to each of their own hay stuffed cots, the prisoners shifted to Skye's arrival. Only six were left who refused his offer.

Skye took his time. "Alright boys, it's about that time." His voice was soft and gentle. "If it means anything coming from a no-good pirate, I respect you few more than you know. Although, I wish you'd reconsider one last time."

A Watchmen spit at Skye's feet. "No, it *doesn't* mean anything, coming from the likes of you."

"I understand. Boys, please escort them out to the docks." Skye tipped his hat and exited.

The prisoners were brought to the dock. A small, ten-men rowboat was prepared. Mounted on it, one sail, along with oars. He ordered the prisoners on to the boat.

"This is my final offer. You know my terms. And after that decent meal last night, I hope you know my heart. Does anyone else wish to join me?"

Ugly stares were their reply.

"Very well…"

"I'll join!" one yelled.

Skye smiled as the other Watchmen cursed their traitor's name. He was released and brought off the boat.

"You know my terms. You will earn your place and if you betray us, your fate will be far worse than dying out at sea. Do you understand?"

"Aye…Captain." The man replied, before joining the other recruits.

"I am at an impasse. I cannot let you share our location just as I do not wish to end your lives. So, I will leave it up to the sea. *One* last chance."

The sailor stood silent. Skye nodded. His men kicked the boat as they untied it from the dock. The full sail was free to drift away. Skye watched for long moments then walked off the dock to shore. Knee deep in water, he submerged his hands and closed his eyes.

"Guagala, we have men passing your cave. These men serve the same who seek to rule your seas. Greed and other selfish desires poison their minds. I have tried to sway them to serve me, to serve *us*. Do what you will with them. My only wish is that you make it quick and painless. They are brave and for that, they have earned the mark of valor. But I'm afraid, they are past saving."

Skye never enjoyed watching what happened next and so he kept his eyes shut. Unlike his men who sat, excited to see the giant waves rise and forcefully crash the boat against the jagged rocks in the corner of the cove. A full minute passed; nothing happened. The prayer Skye had told many times before, took seconds before the water would move in response. Skye opened his eyes. The boat had passed the cave, now free from the cove's clutches yet trapped in the vast ocean.

Placing his hands back in the water he tried to communicate.

"Guagala? You there?"

Still nothing.

"Huh?" Skye's bottom lip curled, and his shoulders shrugged. "Well, if it is your wish they live. Who am I to say?

"Looks like the goddess of the sea has other plans for them." Skye yelled to his men. "Perhaps nothing so great as a quick death."

"She is not a goddess," Marx shouted behind him.

"Marx? What are you doing here? I thought you were leaving today," Skye said.

Marx studied Skye's face. "You don't know?"

"Don't know what?"

"Guagala destroyed that ship she was so nice to give me. With all of us on board." Marx gestured to Elet, Kara and Ethen.

"Why did she do that?" Skye asked.

"Never mind that. That means you still have a debt to pay Elet. She has been patient with you these last days. She needs to get up that strait. You're the reason she's here, far further than she paid you for. Will you not hold true your deal?" Marx said firmly.

Amused, Skye grinned. His men gathered. "You should tame your tone. Don't fool yourself, you're only concerned about one thing." Skye pushed his lips together, mimicking a kiss. His men laughed.

Marx hardened face hardened more as he stepped to Skye; Skye accepted the challenge, walking to meet him. Skye's men ran to protect their captain.

"You gonna have your men fight for you?" Marx's hand rested on his hilt.

"They won't have the chance, with the time I'll need to set you straight." Skye freed his cutlass instantly, like a cracked whip.

"Skye, stop this! Marx is right," Phin interrupted. "You owe the lady a debt."

"And I never said I wouldn't help her. This one needs to be taught manners," Skye's eyes never left Marx.

"I'm not the one who needs to be taught manners. You mocked me and the lady," Marx said, meeting the gaze with his own.

An arrow flew, striking Skye's cutlass out of his hand.

"*I know you are, but what I am. But he started it,*" Elet erupted, lowering her bow. "I swear you two grown men are acting like children. Marx, I appreciate it, but I can take care of myself. Skye…" Elet's next arrow notched swiftly "…so how is it you plan to get me home?"

"I don't know. I only just found out that you still needed a way. Will you not give me a moment to think?" Skye eyed Elet before picking up his sword and sheathing it.

"Nice shot, Elet," Kara praised.

"Look, I apologize." Marx raised his hands. "I've been rattled ever since that lying snake almost killed us all."

"Who? Guagala? What did she lie about?" Skye asked.

"She is no god. I proved that when I cut out her tongue and when she fled. Look at those men you just let go. I imagine you had different plans for them. She is an Ancient. One who served Listar before his fall. Powerful in magic, yes but divine, no. She has been lying to you," Marx said.

Skye looked toward the cave shrouded in fog.

"You cut out her tongue?" Skye asked.

"Yes, which means I have limited her magic, but she's still dangerous I'm sure."

"Phin, what do you make of all this?" Skye asked.

"I have heard of the Ancients, only from lore," Phin answered.

"Ancient whatever or goddess, Guagala has aided me in the past. You suggest I betray her?" Skye asked.

"I only ask you make good on your agreement with Elet. Aid us off this island and up the northern strait," Marx said.

"Whether you know it or not," Phin chimed in. "you *are* asking Skye to betray Guagala. She will not forgive this and therefore Skye will most likely become an enemy as well."

"Although you have proven yourself to me, Guagala is an alliance I don't wish to part with," Skye said. "You admitted yourself she is powerful. Will you offer me nothing?"

"So, what is this? A barter decision?" Marx asked.

"More or less, it is," Skye admitted. "You can't expect me to align myself with you willy nilly. I have men and a mission."

"Guagala tried to kill not only me and Elet but Kara and Ethen. How can you count *that* as bringing peace to the world?" Marx pressed.

"You fail to see my point and therefore my dilemma," Skye pointed out.

"No, I don't. I understand." Marx sighed. "You want a promise of something of equal or greater value." Marx gripped his hilt.

Skye shrugged, nodding. "Sorry. Again, it *is* a barter decision, more or less."

"Fine," Marx replied as time for him slowed.

Marx came to Skye, then after to each surrounding pirate, pulling free each cutlass before he returned to face Skye eye to eye. Startled at Marx's sudden closeness, Skye jumped back, grabbing for his sword that wasn't there. With their captain jumping back, the pirates followed, only to find their weapons fall to their feet. Skye bent down to retrieve his blade, looked around at the others doing the same.

"What in the depths was that?" Skye asked.

"My offer; something of greater or equal value."

Chapter Twelve
An Ancient Tale

"How did you?" Skye asked in wonder.

"Not here. Let's go somewhere safe to talk," Marx said.

Hesitant, Skye glanced out to sea, viewing the Watchmen; a black speck against the bright blue. Smiling at the thought of seeing them again, in some place around the world with his cutlass in hand he nodded. Skye led Marx to Kork's small, crashed ship. Marx told his company to wait outside. As for Phin, Skye insisted he join, stating that any business with Skye was business with his two most trusted—Kork and Phin. Marx allowed. Kork was found inside at work.

"I see you didn't take heed my warning," Skye said.

"My ears were on the lookout. What happened? Have a change of heart?" Kork asked.

"Not exactly. It appears Guagala isn't the goddess I was led to believe," Skye said. "At least that's what Marx claims."

"You know my doubts wouldn't argue with that. So, what is she then but an oversized eel?" Kork asked Marx.

"Have you heard of the Ancients?" Marx asked.

"I haven't for at least a hundred or so years." Finger to chin, Kork's bushy eyebrows rose. "Ah, is *that* what she is? I didn't know they still existed. I, as well as the other older races, have believed that they fell with Listar."

"And what exactly is she?" Skye asked.

Kork turned to face the three, as if telling the tale to children. "The story goes, long, long ago, well before Listar's horrible reign and fall, back when he was considered a god of good, the Ancients were his trusted ambassadors. They were granted powerful magics, everlasting life, and each assigned a role. I'm not exactly sure what role they all had, but essentially, they would report to him or act on his behalf.

"During his fight with Nih and Nil, the Ancients turned on him when he was weakened. When they themselves fell to corruption, they showed Listar their unwillingness to serve him when he needed them most. Of course, this enraged the god. With the betrayal he felt, first from the mortals and now his most trusted, one could say this tipped him over the edge even further. However, he regained control, instilling fear in some of them who then swore an unbinding oath, meaning, unbreakable. An oath only a god of Listar's stature could conjure. Although *all* Ancients weren't bought by fear. Some were appalled by what he'd become, swearing alliance with the twins instead. Unfortunately for those who betrayed him, Listar achieved his awful revenge."

"And then there was always the idea that a few either hid or escaped from both the twins and from Listar successfully. But over the years, that was believed to be a myth. If Marx is correct, Maybe Guagala is one of the few who fled."

"My fear, she's not the only one. If more Ancients are still here and are influencing the minds of mortals, they could be one of the reasons for the meaningless wars that you..." Marx turned to Skye. "... are hoping to end. Think of it. The o'rüks—don't they worship a wolf? And Stafnik, an eagle?"

"Hmm, I never thought of that," Kork said. "One Ancient I've heard of was a ferocious war driven wolf. Faraak, I believe, is the name."

"And the mountain dwarves, those I've known most my life, some of them worship Ulkralc, a warthog god," Marx said. "I never thought much of it but in my short life, I've seen more and more turn to him. They've been acting strangely as of late; the last decade or so. If the Ancients *are* the puppeteers, stringing the world to shambles then I have an entirely different reason to travel up the northern strait."

"You intend to visit your dwarven brothers," Phin answered.

"I had another dream last night. I had forgotten it until my walk here from the other side of the island. It was of a warthog trapped inside a home. Inside the home was normal enough; the furniture, nice and clean. There were shelves and a few tables, each filled with porcelain trinkets. The warthog thrashed everything in sight. The cozy home was turned to disaster."

"*Another* dream was it?" Skye's doubt didn't hide itself.

"Yes," Marx answered sharply. "And that first one, I was reminded of this morning before going on board that ship. I spared the details but in it, a sea serpent watched me as I drowned. What I did share, if you remember, was a warning of drowning. That would have been my fate if I didn't receive a warning."

"A warning from who?" Phin asked.

"I believe it was Nih," Marx said.

"And where exactly is the elf god? Why is he allowing this to happen?" Skye asked.

"I don't know. But I felt his aid in my fight with Guagala. Just as I have felt him before. I cannot expect you to understand but I have been given a duty. If I fail, it will lead the world into an even darker state. Something Guagala is now aware of and therefore I need to warn the only ones who might listen. Either way, if I'm right, this could be the cause of the brokenness in the world you aim to fix. If that is truly your desire, then we can help each other. You saw what I was capable of?" Marx said.

"Aye, what allows you such magics? Nih?" Skye asked.

"I'm sorry, I cannot say, but I have given you no reason to think I would betray you. So, I *need* to give *you* a reason not to betray me."

"Fine, keep your secrets. Phin, Kork? What say you?" Skye asked.

"As you know, I never trusted that Guagala in the first place," Kork said.

"Remember Skye, Marx has proven himself, before he knew who you were, other than we faced certain death. He aligned himself with us then, by offering to rescue us," Phin remarked.

"Aye, I remember," Skye admitted. "So, I bring the lady to Stumpford and you to where, exactly?"

"I'm escorting Elet to Lemwven, I can travel from there on foot. *Or* if you want to stick around, you could save me a few days travel. I need to get to Tungsten's Echo. My first stop is there. After I escort Elet, I need to talk to a few friends who keep in contact with the mountain dwarves. I can ask some questions that will reveal my suspicion. Then, if I need to, I can go see my dwarven brothers. It's about a two-three week trip from there. If my suspicions are wrong, I will give you one year of my service. Anything that is within my convictions. But if I'm right, I might be the one asking *you* for help. For the same reason that runs your operation, peace."

"We shall discuss this with some of our other men," Skye said. "I owe them a say in the matter. Also, I know people scattered all throughout Iris, including Tungsten's Echo. Which happens to be the closest."

"Then, it seems, the most practical place to start," Marx said.

"I suppose so. Although I can't imagine it being a good idea to sail right back past Laneloon in the same ship we stole from em," Skye pointed out.

"We can get by them no problem," Kork said nonchalantly.

"Oh?" Skye said.

"Sure, we got something that we've been working just on the other side of the island. It will do just fine," Kork said.

"Something that doesn't whistle or explode?" Phin teased.

"You won't be snickering once I jolt you with what I'm working on," Kork challenged.

"What? A fruit cocktail? Terrified," Phin replied.

"I'll have you know that what I'm referring to, anyone can appreciate, even someone as dimwitted as you, wizard," Kork replied.

"Phin, you spend more time over there than anyone, you don't know what he's talking about?" Skye asked.

"The smoke machine?" Phin guessed.

"No," Kork said.

"More hallucinogens?" Skye tried.

"Also, no," Kork said.

"Well, what is it?" Skye asked.

Kork reached down and pulled on the bottom drawer at his feet.

"You got it hidden in there?" Skye asked suspiciously.

Ignoring the question, Kork pushed the drawer back in, pulled on the next drawer up and started ruffling through random pieces that others would call junk.

"Aha!" Kork revealed a small bottle of blank liquid. "Check out that."

Kork tossed it at Skye who observed it closely.

"What is it?" Skye asked.

"It's paint, obviously," Kork answered.

"Paint? Your crazy invention that the gnomes have been working on is black paint?" Skye asked. "You know, you worry me in your older years."

"This is why I stopped having fun with our contests a while ago," Phin added. "Now it's just sad,"

Kork rolled his large eyes and shook his head. "You numbskulls." He snatched it back from Skye. "It's not just any black paint. Here, let me show you."

He grabbed a banana and carefully poured every last bit of the black liquid over it, covering it completely. He held it in the light. It took a moment to realize; it showed no third dimension. No light bounced off of it. Like a cutout piece of paper, all that it showed was its two-dimensional, curved, banana shape.

"I must admit, that's impressive," Phin said.

"Yeah, in the dead of night, with the moons and stars out, any ship covered with this will easily slip on by from, let's say, a ship only a few feet away," Kork said impressed with the idea.

"So, you plan to paint an entire ship with this paint?" Skye asked.

"Don't be silly," Kork said. "We only need to paint the right side."

"Back to Guagala. Kork, Phin, you really think she's one of these Ancients?" Skye asked.

"It would make sense out of what she is. Ancients were large, powerful beast-like beings," Kork said.

"Allow me to try to have a word with our turtle friends," Phin said.

"The torques?" Marx asked.

"Yes. I can speak with them in the language of magic," Phin said. "I can find out more about Guagala and about these other Ancients."

"Aren't they aligned with her?" Marx asked.

"I don't know. She may have had them under some spell for all I know. But even if they are aligned with her, I can find out more. They aren't the most cunning of creatures," Phin replied.

"Aye, I'd like to know more about her aim," Skye agreed. "We don't know she won't attack our ships now. Just be careful."

"I'll be fine." Phin replied as he exited Kork's shack and walked to the water.

"We just can't seem to get rid of you," Rifi said to Kara and Ethen.

"You shoulda saw it Rifi, we saw Marx in action," Ethen said excitedly. "First, he threw all of us to shore while we were way out at sea. Then he got swallowed by this giant snake and he cut her tongue out. Oh, and then, in a split second, he disarmed all of Skye's men."

"Yeah, I wouldn't want to be on his bad side. Which reminds me, he thought *you* betrayed him," Kara added. "Did you?"

"It did cross my mind but then it uncrossed," Rifi said. "So, what's next?"

"Not sure, Marx is still trying to get Elet up the strait, and I think he offered Skye to join him when he showed off his speed trick," Kara said.

"What's he doing?" Ethen pointed at Phin who was waist deep in the ocean.

"Beats me," Rifi said.

"Him catch fish fish bites?" Kagu guessed.

After a moment of watching him, they saw a torque's head pop up ten feet away, then another and finally a third.

"Doesn't he know how dangerous they are?" Kara said as she walked forward.

"Hold on." Ethen grabbed her. "I think he's talking to them."

The four stood and watched him for several minutes until he made his way back. Marx, Skye and Kork walked out as he approached.

"So, what'd they say?" Skye asked.

"They are thankful," Phin said to Marx. "They were indeed under Guagala's spell, and you freed them. She appeared defeated in many ways. Although she is still powerful, she does not pose a great threat." Phin turned to Skye. "She is not the god she said she was."

"Told ya," Kork said.

"Actually, Marx told me. Well, either way, she helped me more than not and so I don't feel too cheated." Skye shifted to Marx. "The bigger picture, this gives your theory a bit more credit. I must admit, she had some influence over my decisions more and more over these past few years. And if there are more of these beings, and they have the same power and influence, then they could sway kings and lords. So, maybe you're not as crazy as you sound.

"We should gather our men for a meeting and then go collect that black paint…" Skye was interrupted.

A shock boomed. The entire ocean shook and rippled. In wonder, they all watched the waves wobble and raise, then lower. Steady ripples covered the vast surface. A few small fish popped out from the water before a few larger ones followed. Then all sorts of sea creatures emerged from all over: dolphins, torques, octopi, and sharks. Even giant whales burst up briefly.

"What in the…" Kara asked.

"Phin, what was that?" Skye asked.

"I have no idea."

"Do you think it was Guagala?"

"With her power diminished, I don't see how."

"Whatever it was, it spoke to me." Skye was locked onto the sea.

"That was scary," Ethen admitted.

"I'd be lying if I said I wasn't shaken," Kork said.

"Aye, me too," Skye added.

"As am I," Marx agreed. "I've never felt such a power."

"Yeah, that was really weird," Kara said.

"The sea speaks," Skye studied the rippling waters, then turned back to the others. "We need answers, and I aim to get some from my own sources up north," Skye said. "We'll resupply at Rimcaster, sneak past Laneloon and then up the strait."

"Finally," Elet said.

"What about that big snakey thing?" Ethen asked.

"If Marx cut out her tongue, I'll go for her eyes if she moves on me or my men," Skye returned coolly. "Either way, she'll no longer influence my direction, and that starts with this moment."

"Let's not forget the paint," Kork reminded.

"Aye, and I'll need to borrow some *working* black powder from your kin as well, just in case. We'll have a chat with the men, but we cannot sit idle; I know it. We should leave by dusk." Skye turned to Marx. "Congratulations—looks like you have yourself a ship and a crew."

Thank you for reading the pulp edition—the first of three books that come together to form my upcoming novel, **Temple of Lost Tears**. I hope you enjoyed it, and if you did, there is much more to look forward to such as Book II & III as well as the novel itself. The full novel will include maps, art, extra chapters, the written rules to the dice game Dead Kraken (mentioned in Chapter 3) and even a sneak peek to the next novel,

Temple of Hidden Blood.

As a self-published author, your help is very appreciated. If you can, leave an honest review and if you'd like to check out my earlier work, I wrote a throwback to the classics like Alice in Wonderland and Peter Pan, **The Abstract Adventures of Jacob Knots**.

You can follow me now by joining my newsletter at **nixplots.com** to keep up on my next projects.

Until the next adventure, read on.

-Nic-

About the Author

Nicholaus Hutton never really planned to write about pirates or far-off worlds, but once the stories started showing up inside his mind, he didn't have much choice. Somewhere between quiet mornings sipping coffee with his dog Dapper, late-night edits, and life on the road across the States, worlds began to take shape.

When he isn't crafting tales that twist the familiar into the fantastic, Nic can be found tucked inside his van, surrounded by books, journals, and just enough space for his thoughts to wander. His writing often dances between whimsy and wonder, faith and doubt, and the strange beauty found when both worlds meet.

Nicholaus is the author of *The Abstract Adventures of Jacob Knots*, a story that blends imagination and heart in equal measure. His upcoming works continue to explore the vast landscapes of fantasy, each one layered with mystery, humor, and a desperate sense of hope.

If you ever catch him staring out at a sunset too long, he's probably building another world in his head, and he'll gladly invite you in

Made in the USA
Las Vegas, NV
21 October 2025